HOMELESS

THE DOLLMAKER'S WEB

A Novella

J. KECK

Other works by J. Keck:

The Big House - Story of a Southern Family
    Volumes 1 and 2

*Dedicated to
My Family and Friends*

CHAPTER ONE

Thursday, February 2

The flight from Switzerland to L.A. arrived late in the morning. I had just enough time after customs and baggage, the drive home, and a change of clothes to get to the clinic for my first appointment. I was an intern counseling people in the mid-1980s.

A woman in her late twenties came into the building at the end of the day and asked to speak with "someone, anyone." Because I was the only one there to talk with, Jennifer was soon sitting across from me. Blonde and lean, with blue eyes that moved back and forth anxiously, she didn't wait for me to ask the first question—she lurched forward.

"I left my husband and children for another . . . woman!"

She paused slightly, then declared, "I told Todd about Joan. The next day, he told my dad and his own family." She sank back into the chair and closed her eyes. Breathing out, she said softly, "His family told others and pretty soon, the whole town knew. That's just the way it is back there."

Jennifer looked up and gazed vacantly at the ceiling for a time. A sound outside the door evidently reminded her of where she was. She focused back on me and sighed, "None of 'em want anything to do with me. So, I left. I left town with her."

At that moment, she looked desperate, alone and out of place, huddled in the old, overstuffed chair that had been donated either by someone or—more likely—by the nearby thrift store.

She closed her eyes, pressed her lips together, then opened them slowly and added, "The town's really small, less than 500 folks. A couple of churches, a bank, a school and a few shops. Oh, yeah," she hesitated, "there's a bar named The Firewater Saloon, where a lot of the ranch hands hang out. Joan thought the name was 'corny,' but then, she didn't much like the town or the townspeople. I guess, you'd say . . . well, she just sort of tolerated us."

"Sounds like that kind of hurt your feelings?"

Caught up in telling her story, Jennifer hurried along. "Anyway, she was just visitin' one of her relatives. We met one day at the general store in town. We spent part of the summer getting to know each other. She started to come out to the ranch and have dinner with us. After a while, she'd stay overnight. Then it wasn't long before she'd be there for days at a time. Finally, it just happened.

"You know, *it* just happened," she repeated, looking at me searchingly.

"The two of you became lovers," I said matter-of-factly.

"Uh huh." She looked down and began to twist the button on her faded shirt. Dressed in blue jeans, she came from the flatlands of southern Colorado at the foot of the Rocky Mountains. She had the wholesome good looks and simple, direct demeanor of people from the ranchlands of the West.

I waited, giving Jennifer the time she needed to know she had been heard and understood. Her gaze returned to me ever so slightly, and I wondered to myself if she were trying to assess if it was safe, or even worthwhile, to continue speaking with me—a man.

"She comes from California," Jennifer started, "even though she's got some family in Colorado. She comes from California," she said, repeating herself. "Big difference," shaking her head. "There's a real big difference. Californians are friendly and all, but not really to be counted on. They'll say one thing and mean another. You find that out soon enough.

"When I came home yesterday, my suitcase was on the doorstep. A scrap of paper was taped to the side." She reached into her breast pocket and pulled out a note and read it. "I'm not in love with you anymore. You need to go. Sorry, Joan"

She waited, seemingly collecting her thoughts, then she said absently, "'Sorry'. That's all!? That's all she wrote . . . just 'sorry'." Jennifer's chest heaved once. She caught her breath; she appeared to stifle the need to cry.

"I have nowhere to go. No one—just no one—wants me."

"You said your husband told your dad, but maybe—"

"No!" she interrupted. "My mom died when I was fifteen. Cancer. Then it was just me and him, my dad, out on the ranch." Jennifer shook her head adamantly. "No, that jus' won't work. Anyway, my husband, he's there, too. And, he's got the kids."

"Your children, what are their names?"

"I have three of 'em, all boys. Jamie, the youngest, he's three; William's five; and Michael, he's the oldest at seven."

With the mention of Michael's name, I saw Jennifer's expression change. It softened and she seemed to become almost

5

reflective. "Michael, he's your first—the oldest?" I asked.

"Yeah. I missed his birthday last week. I sent a card, but I don't know if he'll even get it. We were always very close. I hope—" Jennifer stopped.

"Well, like I said, we all lived with him—my dad—out there. My husband had a part-time job in town and also worked on the ranch. Before that, before I was married, I used to work with my dad and take care of the house. Once I had the kids, it was all cookin', washin', lookin' after 'em, and all the rest you gotta do. Everything changed. I never had time to get out on a horse to help round up the strays anymore.

"Anyway," Jennifer said stoically, "My dad's a real churchgoer. When he found out . . . well, that night he just sat there at the kitchen table and wouldn't talk to me. He just kept noddin' at the door.

"I guess I didn't understand. Finally, he said, 'Satan's gotcha. Ya ain't no good, daughter. Ya brought shame on us—on your whole family. Go on, git out! Go!' He stood up. His body was shakin'. He was shouting at me, 'Go t' that whore! Now, git yer things and git out'a here! Now! And don't ya go lookin' for the kids. They're out'a ya reach—some place safe. Ya ain't gettin' yer hands on them kids an' corruptin' 'em. Git out! Ya're no damn good. Ya hear me? Git out!!'"

I realized that the words of both her father's, "Get out!" and Joan's, "I don't love you anymore. Sorry," were not being repeated in anger by Jennifer. Anger could have provided her with the motivation to fight back. Without anger and indignation, these words were like arrows that had pierced a suit of armor, leaving her bleeding, unable to defend herself. With no support, she lay defenseless, lacking hope and—quite possibly—even the will to survive.

"What do you plan to do? Where are you staying tonight?"

She sat there, showing little emotion. I could sense her rising anxiety by the movement of her hands—slowly folding and unfolding the tissue on her lap. I watched as she began to tear and shred the tissue into long, narrow little streamers. Still, her face seemed frozen and impassive.

"Last night, I was on the street. I will *not* live like that—like some sort of animal." She shook her head slowly and said darkly, "I swear to God, I jus' won't live like that!" She looked into my eyes. "I have nowhere to go. No one wants me anymore," Jennifer said despondently, her voice trailing off as she looked away.

"I'm wondering if you might be feeling like you want to hurt yourself?"

Jennifer's gaze came back to rest on mine briefly and, without saying a word, she broke eye contact and looked over at the wall. I could see she was clenching her jaw. I had a sense of foreboding, but nothing had been said by her that would allow me to have her put under observation for a State psychiatric evaluation.

I reviewed my options and said, "Wait here, let me see if I can find a place for you to stay." What I did not say was, "at least for the night," because the shelters were bursting at the seams with the homeless.

As I began to stand, she said in a hushed voice, "No, don't bother. It doesn't matter now." She gripped the arms of the chair and began to push herself up.

"Yes, yes, it does matter." I stood up and said softly, but firmly, "Please, wait for me here." She slowly lowered herself back onto the chair.

I left the room, searched the Rolodex file at the front desk, called the few facilities around, and found no vacancies. I asked the volunteer at the desk if he knew of some place, but he was at a loss to help. Finally, I dialed the only number left, a hospice. I knew calling there was dicey—not only was it not intended for the homeless, the facility was understaffed and underfunded. I asked the manager for help.

"Yes, send her over. We have a room. You know, there are only men here, but . . . if she wants to come—"

The man on the other end of the line sounded rushed, so I told him without really knowing, "She's coming, now."

I came back into the room and gestured positively, "I have a place for you and . . . you'll have your own room."

Jennifer nodded, got out of her chair, and we walked out of the room. "You're my last patient." Assuming she had no car, as she was carrying her suitcase with her coat slung over it, I said, "I'll drive you over there. Let's go."

As we walked past the volunteer at the desk, he asked, "Evan, do you—"

I glanced at him and shook my head. Without comment, the volunteer placed the donation envelope onto the pile of empty envelopes next to the phone. There would be no money from this session. It was *pro bono*, again.

Once we were in the car, I explained that all the shelters were full, but in my desire not to provoke more anxiety in her I quickly added, "We're lucky. A sort of medical place has both a bed and a private room for you." We drove on in silence for some time.

The flight from Zurich and rush to the clinic left me running on nervous energy. As I was driving, I questioned how the seminar at the Jungian Institute could help me. I already had my doubts. At this moment, dream analysis and archetypes seemed obtuse and irrelevant to the immediacy of the needs of my patients. Drug, alcohol, spousal and child abuse were foremost in case management sessions and, now with the AIDS crisis, a siege mentality had gripped patient and healthcare provider alike, as the losses continued to mount during the epidemic. There was still so little known about the disease.

I pulled up and parked the car in front of an old brick building on a busy street in a run-down part of town. The building, a modest hotel from the thirties and forties, had slid quietly into a haven for the downright poor and elderly over the last couple of decades until, finally, it had reached its nadir as a flophouse for druggies and prostitutes.

Now, unnoticed, it had experienced a resurrection in the early years of the AIDS epidemic. New owners made an attempt to spruce it up with paint on the trim and door; nonetheless, the building had a somewhat pathetic look, almost one of sadness. It reminded me in an odd way of some of the old men, wearing their self-ironed and out-of-date suits, wandering the downtown streets alone, with nothing to do and nowhere special to go.

"As I said, we're lucky to get the room." Not looking at Jennifer, I pushed the bell and waited. "The fellas in residence," I continued, "they're good men, just . . . just not doing so well . . . they're kinda in transition." I turned to look at her to see her reaction. She stood there, unmoving, her face still impassive and without expression.

I pressed the bell again. "Some are sicker than others, not mentally and not because of drug addiction." I peered at her earnestly to see her reaction. Again, there was none, nothing discernible.

"They've got AIDS," I declared bluntly. "Some aren't showing the outward signs; others are just getting by at best."

Jennifer looked over at me silently. Then I watched her gaze move to the door and slowly up the face of the building, to linger on the lighted window on the second floor, over the door. Finally, it came back to rest on me again.

I saw that her pale blue eyes were empty of all emotion now. Earlier, in the office, she was agitated and anxious; now her eyes were still and unmoving, like the surface of a swimming pool on a windless day. She made an attempt at a smile— ironic, I wondered—but it faded almost as quickly as it appeared.

Jennifer said simply, "How long can I stay?"

Before I could answer, the door opened. A man in his late thirties with thinning brown hair and of medium height stood in front of a dimly-lit stairwell. "Who are you?" he said impatiently.

"Evan. I called a few minutes, ago. You said you could—"

"Yes, yes, I know."

"This is Jennifer." Before I could finish speaking, he was already turning away.

"C'mon in. I've got people upstairs who need me."

"Jennifer, I'll come by and see you tomorrow, about six, six in the evening," I said.

We looked at the manager of the hospice to see what he would say. "Yeah, if she wants to, she can stay. Room's empty, for now," he called back, as he plodded up the stairs.

Jennifer followed the manager with her suitcase in hand. For all of his impatience, I noticed he took each stair slowly and, it seemed, almost reluctantly. I felt the weight of this forlorn place reaching out toward me with its silent reproach to my own good fortune. "I have a home, a family, and good health," I thought.

I stood there until they reached the second floor landing and disappeared into the building. I closed the door, went back to my car, and drove off. Approaching car lights and the street lamps became blurry. What had been a fine mist earlier became a heavy drizzle and the window was wet. I turned on the wipers and saw a street person huddled in one of the doorways of a closed shop, with a piece of plastic pulled up to his chin. I was relieved that Jennifer was not out here, too.

I went home, documented my session with the new patient, then reviewed and organized my notes for the meeting with my supervisor early tomorrow morning. Dr. Rauchenberg, born and educated in Berlin, was known as "Der Preusser," the Prussian, by German speakers. He was strict, disciplined, and methodical. A good theoretician of various psychological disciplines, he demanded that an intern be thoroughly grounded in his chosen model and demonstrate a clear, logical rationale for his treatment plan. Few interns wanted Rauchenberg as their supervisor.

I looked over my notes and prepared myself for the obvious question: why had I sent a depressed woman, alone, with nowhere to go, to a hospice? Rather than construct a clinical rationale for my decision, I decided the best response was simple. With no shelter, support system, family, friends, or money, and with her anxious-depressed mood, the hospice at least offered her temporary security. That's as good as it gets, I thought.

Coping with jet lag, I lay in my bed, thinking about why else I might be awake. One thing, I thought, was the obvious culture shock: Switzerland, snow, *wurst und senf,* hot sausages and mustards at outdoor grills on carts in Benele Vue Platz; the smell of fresh bread and taste of *Schlagrahm,* thick whipped cream on pastries; and the sound of German with the occasional French or English. All of that was instantly swept away by a transatlantic flight and the casual lifestyle of Southern California.

My thoughts eventually drifted to the warm, green days of the previous summer, thumbing rides and hiking in Bavaria and the Alps. I blotted out the cold and damp of winter in this part of the world, to that moment standing outside Amsberg, a small Bavarian town, waiting in the sunshine with my thumb out, when a caravan of three Volkswagen vans rolled by me on the narrow road leading out of town. Young women yelled and waved at me. The last van stopped and the door opened. A hand reached out, waving me toward them.

I smiled to myself, remembering what I soon found out to be college girls, a soccer club on the way to the dense Bohemian Forest, and a long weekend of play, beer, and singing. My gear was shoved into the van with theirs. I climbed in, shoulder-to-shoulder, and thigh-to-thigh. Spirits were high as we rolled off. One young fellow with fourteen young women. I had been invited to come along and readily agreed.

CHAPTER TWO

Friday, February 3

The next evening, I stopped at the hospice. As I stood before the door, I was annoyed with myself for not having checked earlier to confirm that Jennifer was still there. I waited. I rang the bell again, and—almost simultaneously—the door opened and the manager stood there. "What."

It was not the sound of a question but more of a statement of fact, as there was no inflection in his voice. His flannel shirt was halfway unbuttoned, exposing much of his chest; his pants, obviously too long, were gathered up around his ankles. His appearance was disheveled. However, it was the dark circles and puffiness under his eyes that suggested to me he had not slept much, if at all, the previous night.

"I came by to see Jennifer and to talk with her."

"Upstairs. In her room. This way."

Without another word, he turned. This time I followed behind him. When he began to speak again, I noticed his words had a slightly hollow sound because the ceiling above the stairs was high and reached the second floor.

"Been there all day in her room, except to come out for lunch. Didn't want to sit down at the table with the guys. Just wanted to take a sandwich back to her room." He shook his head adamantly. "I told her she couldn't, 'cause it isn't allowed. So she sat down, but didn't say much, ate, and went back to her room."

When we reached the top of the stairs, he turned to face me and shrugged. He tapped his forehead with his finger. "Who knows what's goin' on in there?" He tilted his head toward a closed door at the end of the hall. "She's in there, in her room," and walked away.

Someone faintly called out his name, "Bernard, Bernard, help me! help me. Ohhh—"

I listened to an agonizing groan, followed by the same voice, pleading, "Ohhh gawd, it's the pain. Please help me, Bernard."

I watched Bernard disappear into one of the rooms, heard a muffled cry, then Bernard say consolingly, "It's all right. I'm here. I'm right here next to you . . . over here . . . on your other side, Gary. Here, squeeze my hand. It's O.K."

I listened to what had become an indistinguishable soft murmur of voices. I thought about my own initial impression of Bernard—his brusque, almost rude, seemingly uncaring behavior, his slovenly appearance tonight and, now, this same man (with the tender voice) nursing a dying, frightened man who lay in darkness, in pain, and in despair.

As I stood there, I felt somewhat guilty for my earlier judgment of Bernard. I took a deep breath and collected my thoughts, then walked over to the closed door at the end of the hall and knocked softly.

I hesitated. I was about to knock again when the door slowly opened.

Jennifer stood in front of me. She had changed her clothes from the previous night. Blue jeans and a plaid shirt with stud buttons—like you'd see on a cowboy—fitted her lean frame snugly. The clothes were clean and they were ironed.

"Hi," I said.

"Hi," she said in a whisper.

Jennifer turned, went over to the bed and sat down, staring at the floor. I pulled a wooden chair closer to the bed. I let myself down gingerly on the seat, since the legs wobbled. As I pulled the patient file and a pen out of my briefcase, Jennifer blurted out, "She wants to kill me!"

Startled, and at a momentary loss for words, I heard her say again with a growing sense of urgency, "She wants to kill me!"

"Who wants to kill you?" I looked up, the file still unopened.

Jennifer jerked up from the bed, took a few steps, twirled, and confronted me, "I said . . . I said *she* wants to kill me!"

"I can hear you saying that *she* wants to kill you. What is her name—the one who wants to kill you?"

Jennifer was apparently stunned—momentarily speechless—by my question. Then she said, slightly annoyed, "Joan. I already told you about her. Joan, the one who left me, put my bag in front of the door. Her!" Jennifer came back, slowly sat down on the edge of the bed, and leaned slightly forward, her long blonde hair slipping partially across her shoulders.

"Joan!" She said with emphasis. "She wants to kill me!" Now the tone of her voice dropping ominously as she said urgently, "She *killed* the last two women who lived with her."

I felt the impact of her words: *She killed,* and was conscious that my brow furrowed as I tried to process the unlikely reality of murder and the probability of major depression with a psychotic break.

I said cautiously, "You're saying that Joan—" There was a pause as I prepared my response, "Joan—"

Jennifer picked up on the direction of my unspoken question and responded quickly, saying, "She didn't kill them. She *made* them commit suicide."

"How did she . . . how did Joan make them commit suicide?" I asked tentatively.

"I saw their pictures," she stammered. "She even kept their licenses—their driver's licenses in her photo album, along with other little things, like a cuttin' of their hair, tied with a small ribbon. Even pieces of cloth that looked jus' like what they were wearin' in the pictures. You know, the albums, they were that big cloth kind with the plastic that you can fold over the pictures. She even had—"

"You said," I brought the subject back to suicide, "that she made them commit suicide. How did Joan make them commit suicide?" I asked carefully.

Jennifer had stood up and was pacing now. Her white sneakers looked new and clean against the shabby carpet, which was stained and worn. The strong smell of the carpet was insistent and began to draw my attention, when I realized that Jennifer had stopped at the sagging curtains and was staring at the window pane. There was the sound of raindrops striking the glass, at first one at a time, then—unexpectedly— the beat increased quickly until there was a cascade of water flowing relentlessly down the glass. I noticed that my attention wandered as I recalled a similar image in a painting by the French Impressionist, Édouard Manet.

Waiting for her response, I became aware of sounds now above and around me. They seemed to be coming from inside the walls. I looked over at Jennifer, gazing at me and my confusion.

"Rats . . . they're rats." She nodded toward the wall and lifted her eyes upward. "They're crawling inside the walls. You hear 'em mostly at night—like now.

"We used to have 'em at the ranch," she said dryly. "Not in the house, of course.

The cats and dogs took care of that; but they were in the barn."

For the first time, I saw her grin. Jennifer shook her head and her hair, catching the light, swayed back and forth as she remembered. The sadness in her eyes, though, seemed to convey an expression of someone reviewing the distant past, almost another life.

"Some mornings the cats would leave a couple of 'em at the door, just to show us, I guess, that they were earning their keep."

The mixed feelings evoked with the recollection were quickly extinguished by the reality of her circumstances. The uncovered bulb bore down from the ceiling overhead relentlessly and cast a hard glare, creating dark shadows where none would be found in a room with lamps. Jennifer's eyes now seemed sunken, the high cheekbones of her face sculpted by darkness. Her wide, full lips looked thin and severe in the harsh light.

"Jennifer," I said, "tell me, have you been thinking about committing suicide yourself?"

"Well, I have been tellin' you that she wants me to. You know," she then said abstractly, "your eyes are green," and she looked at me as if she were seeing me for the first time. "Your eyes are the same color as Joan's."

Interpreting Jennifer's remark about the color of my eyes as avoidance, some type of evasive maneuver, I persisted with my question. "Jennifer, have *you* been thinking about it—thinking about committing suicide yourself? Do you have a plan?"

"I—" said Jennifer wearily, dropping her head, "No, I can't talk anymore t'night, O.K.?" The question at the end of her statement was not, I suspected, an opening for discussion. It was a respectful request to terminate the session. "I'm jus' real tired and let's jus' say I'm thankful that I've got a bed to sleep in, t'night. I think God must've been lookin' out for me."

Listening to the scratching of the rats inside the walls around us, I agreed it was time to end our session. "Yes. Why don't we wrap up for tonight? It's already Friday. I'll come back Monday . . . at six in the evening."

I paused a moment, reaching into my briefcase, "Here's a notebook and pencil. You might want to try writing down some of your feelings about what has happened to you, or anything else that comes into your head." Stressing the feeling side, I said, "How you feel about it: 'I feel sad about' . . . 'I am angry about . . . whatever—"

I looked at her to see if she understood what I was saying. Was she able to track my instructions? Holding her gaze and seeing her reach out her hand to take the material, I continued. "Whatever comes into your mind, write it down. Any time of day or night. There are no rules of grammar or spelling. Just write, O.K.?"

She nodded affirmatively.

I stood up and went to the door, then turned back cautiously. Jennifer was standing in the same place, obviously still agitated and tense. Her hands were clutched together in front of her chest, giving the impression of someone desperately praying. I could hear her breathing as her chest rose and fell. She stared at me, unspeaking.

"I'll be here Monday at six." I turned, opened the door, and walked into the hall. As I closed the door behind me, I stopped and looked back. "I'll see you Monday at six, O.K.?"

Jennifer nodded again and I closed the door, hoping she'd be there Monday.

That night, I tossed and turned. The intensity of the session left me disturbed and restless. I started to go over the events of our meeting, but realized it did not bring any relief from my doubts about her condition. After a while, I stared out into the room and saw the outlines of the frame of a painting, partially illuminated by the gibbous moon. Though I was unable to see its mountain scenery, my mind wandered to the Bohemian Forest and to the van as it broke through the low cloud cover.

. . . . .

The VW made a quick turn, and Evan saw the chalet standing there among the trees. He could decipher the Gothic script just above the door: *Die Waldhuette,* the Forest Chalet. A room was found for Evan; actually, more a large closet. A mattress was placed on the floor, reaching from the side wall to the armoire. Within inches of the foot of the mattress was a small window, around which a dense, green vine had been neatly trimmed. The shared bathroom was down the hall.

It was a sweltering day. The women played soccer throughout the afternoon, until a men's soccer club from a nearby local town checked in and wanted to share the turf. The women decided it was time to shower, as it was a community shower. Earlier arriving, more affluent guests had already taken the few rooms with private baths. The women's club insisted the American not be a prude and shower with them. During the shower, Evan saw them whispering. Somewhat embarrassed, he got up his courage to teasingly ask, looking down at himself, if American men were all that different from Germans.

Ruth, one of the women who traveled in the front seat of the van earlier that morning, asked Evan innocently—but directly—if he were Jewish. When he replied, no, she then asked why he was cut. He explained that it was generally customary for the majority of American males to be *bescheidet,* circumcised, at birth.

He reached down and pulled on his penis—he noticed he had their full attention—and mimicked with the two fingers of his other hand a pair of scissors. *Snip*, and he grimaced in mock pain, "*Oh, Weh!* Oh, Ouch!" which initially stunned the group, leaving them speechless. For a moment, he gulped and thought he had possibly embarrassed both them and himself.

Then Ruth started to laugh. Evan was relieved. All of them now laughed, including Evan. He knew he had broken a barrier and became, at some level, part of the group.

As they were toweling off, Ruth explained in rather good English that tomorrow evening they would all eat together and celebrate in the dining hall. He noticed that her eyes were not black, but an incredibly dark blue—much like a cabochon sapphire, releasing its blue flame once a beam of light hit its smooth, non-faceted surface.

Ruth saw Evan's fascination—like most men—with her eyes. He had completely forgotten she was nude. She smiled and said that she saw his eyes were green, a very beautiful green, which made him blush, amusing Ruth. She said nonchalantly that he looked German; Alpine German, with his blond hair and—she looked down casually—with his powerful legs. He "fit in," she said, were it not for the color of his eyes.

Evan, disarmed, volunteered picking up the conversation in English; that her explanation of the German part of him was accurate, at least his father's half. His mother, who was of Dutch and Scottish descent—the green eyes came from the Scots. Jokingly, he said that like the majority of Americans, he was a mutt. He could see that Ruth did not understand the word, so switching back to German he settled on *der Koeter.*

He was startled to see Ruth cringe and shrink back reflexively from the term, leaving him to wonder if he had said something that confirmed an old stereotype of many Americans as half-breeds. It was then that he remembered the literal translation of the word as 'cur,' so he quickly said *gemischt,* mixed, which brought about her audible sigh of relief. Her belated expression of amusement reminded him that German was not his mother tongue.

That evening, exhausted from the drive from Munich and from the games, the girls kept to themselves in their rooms and ate from their supplies, ostensibly saving their money for Saturday night. Evan ate alone among the few other guests. The older waitress was cheerful, but after the day's events, the evening was a bit of a letdown for him. Not even the common room or main hall with its wood paneling, huge ceiling beams and blazing fireplace, once a hunting lodge for nobility, impressed him. The warm, cozy atmosphere only reinforced his sense of separation from the high-spirited girls upstairs.

CHAPTER THREE

Monday, February 6

Friday's on-again, off-again rain became a full storm that lasted the weekend and through all of Monday. This winter, one storm was closely followed by another and the streets, particularly the intersections, were flooded. Getting to the hospice was a hassle and I was annoyed with myself, again, for not having called in advance to be sure that Jennifer was still there.

I rang the bell and waited in the rain. I stood there and thought about the news that day at the facility—a young man (a patient of mine with AIDS) had shot and killed himself over the weekend. A creative and productive artist, he was aware of growing dementia that was destroying his ability to maintain himself and control his life. I remembered the last thing he said to me on Friday as he walked away: "It's going to be a difficult weekend." I realized I needed to process my feelings about his death—the personal loss and the sense of inadequacy, even failure on my part for not anticipating the suicide. Yet I thought, when asked during various sessions, including the last, he had not indicated he was at risk of committing suicide. I decided to stop thinking about the situation until I was in case management, where I could explore the issue in greater depth. Now, especially now, was not the time.

I was aware of the rain coming down even harder when, finally, Bernard opened the door and said curtly, "C'mon in."

He continued to truncate his sentences as we climbed the stairs. "Been better; helped out a lot around here: clearing tables, washin' dishes, all sorts of things. Wasn't even asked to help. Guys like her. Think I'll see if she wants to stay for room and board and a few bucks. Not much money here. Hard enough just to keep the place runnin' and to put food on the table."

Although I knew we were climbing upward, I found myself feeling as if I were entering the underworld: the dim light and the mustiness reminded me of spelunking, snaking along a passage into an underground cavern, the carbide lantern lighting the direction ahead, and the rat droppings on the dirt floor. Rats. Yes, I remembered Jennifer's room.

When we got to the top of the landing, Bernard started to walk away, then abruptly turned and faced me. "Jenny's good. Even spent time in the living room, too, playing checkers with the fellas." His nose wrinkled, but it was quickly followed by a smile, as if he just recalled something amusing. He chortled and appeared ready to talk with me.

I looked searchingly at him and was going to respond, when he walked off. I felt then that he was burned out, resigned to the reality of death and dying. Yet, I could see he still found the energy and resolve to do what he did day after day. Knowing that the sick and helpless depended on him seemed to allow him to draw from some strength deep within himself: he had a purpose.

Back in her room, Jennifer was restless. She was pacing again. There was the unhealthy smell of old curtains and carpet, the sound of the rats scratching and scurrying behind the walls. There was also the sound of heavy rain lashing against the windows. I caught myself again allowing my attention to wander. I thought about— if only fleetingly—the drive home along the flooded streets.

"She wants me to kill myself, just like the other two did. Listen to me," Jennifer pleaded, "I'm not . . . cra . . . zy," returning to sit on the edge of the bed.

Jennifer sat there erect and tense, obsessed with the thought of Joan, staring at me, unflinching, for a long while. Then she looked down at the carpet, almost in despair. "It's weird . . . really. It's true. She wants me to kill myself, I know it," Jennifer repeated.

"It sounds as if you're feeling scared of this power she has. She wants to, I mean, she wants you to harm yourself. You're feeling afraid of what you might do yourself."

"Uh-huh." She looked a little startled that I seemed to "get it."

"Have you thought about hurting yourself?" I said.

"Mmmm, I thought about it. Uh-huh. But then I think about my boys." Jennifer squinted suspiciously and tilted backward. "You know, you keep askin' me about it—jus' like Joan used to. It's strange, really strange."

Bringing her attention back to Joan, she continued. "It's weird; she's weird. She makes dolls. It's—" she shuddered.

My question about Jennifer possibly harming herself triggered a degree of paranoia, indicated by her body language, her fixed, suspicious stare, the flat, guarded tone of her voice, and the visible tilt of her body pulling away from me. Fear—fear was apparent to me. I dropped that line of questioning and came back to Joan's doll-making. "It appears you're really scared about Joan making dolls. I think you said, 'It's weird'," shifting to an empathic response.

Grimacing, she went on. "She has a studio, her garage, where she used to make bowls and things outta clay. Now, she makes dolls' heads and sometimes the hands. Then she bakes." Jennifer stopped herself, momentarily searching for the right term. "She 'fires' them in what she called (I forgot it, the word) in a special oven. Oh yeah, I know. It's called a kiln or something like that.

"Yes, and . . . and—" I could see Jennifer seemed to be hyperventilating, "she takes 'em out and lets 'em cool. Then she paints on their faces and does it again—fires 'em. She gets real hair for 'em, too. She buys it, the cuttings, from barbers and beauty shops. Some of her customers buy a lot of her dolls for their collections. They tell her the real hair makes the dolls more beautiful, more valuable. But the weird part doesn't have to do with those dolls—the ones for her customers. It's the ones she keeps."

Intently searching my face for cues, she anxiously continued. "Remember, I told you about the picture album she has with all the stuff—Janice and Rebecca's licenses, cuttin's of their hair, pictures and other things?"

"Yes, I remember," I said as evenly as possible.

"Well, the faces on the dolls look just like the photos in the album!"

Jennifer, evidently seeing I appeared calm and unmoved by the significance of what she just said, spoke more stridently. "Their hair's the same, the same color, the same texture, as the hair in the album. It's the same . . . it's the same hair. I matched 'em up!

"The clothes, the clothes on the dolls, too, look just like the clothes in some of the pictures."

Finding myself being drawn into the history and the intensity of her feelings, I made a conscious and determined effort to maintain a therapeutic distance. "It sounds as if you felt, and still feel, alarmed by the dolls—how closely they actually resemble the pictures in the album, even including the hair."

Jennifer bore down on the narrative. "She showed me another album with her dead parents' and sister's pictures—they were killed in a car accident when she was ten. Joan said she had to go and live with an aunt and uncle, and he did 'very bad things' to her, but she didn't want to talk about it. Except once, when she said her aunt slapped Joan's face and punished her when she tried to tell her what Uncle Bud was doin' to her. You know, even with that or anything else, she never showed any emotion at all, until—"

"Until?" I said, bending slightly forward and maintaining steady, yet unthreatening eye contact, hoping to encourage her to finish her thought but sensing in her pause an ambivalence or reluctance to disclose more.

"Until we started doin' the puppet shows."

"Puppet shows," I said, trying with some effort not to let my voice rise, since I was somewhat startled by her reply. She continued to explain in detail.

"Every evening for a couple of months, we'd have to do a puppet show. One was about her parents and sister. She had dolls that looked jus' like 'em. We had to, I mean, I had to read the script exactly as she wrote it. (Joan had memorized all the dialogue, so she knew when I didn't do it right.)

"Everything had to be read just as it was written. Otherwise, she would get really irritated with me. She would say, 'Read it just as it's written; you're not doing it right. Your accent is all wrong; you sound like a hick. Stop dropping the endings to words. It's 'coming' with a 'g,' not 'comin'. You should say 'them,' not 'em'. Well, I'd have to go over and over it, until I got it right," said Jennifer in exasperation.

"Joan sounds like a really strict teacher. Sounds as if you were really feeling uptight about not saying the words perfectly—not making any mistakes."

"Yeah. Sometimes I got so nervous I would make even more mistakes. But she wouldn't let me stop 'til we had finished the lines and the play."

Jennifer leaned forward. "She had two other plays: one was about Janice and her, and the other was about Rebecca and her. She always played herself. I got the parts of Janice and Rebecca. At first, I cried during certain parts, but then it got so boring. Also, something jus' didn't seem right about it. Joan would end up cryin' and cryin', always at the same parts, sort of like she knew when. I guess she felt she was allowed to do it then—cry. Because all the rest of the time, she never showed much emotion, even when she seemed to be tryin' to connect with me.

"Anyway, I was readin' the parts— I even rehearsed them during the day—but most of the time she'd still not like the way I read 'em. No matter how hard I tried, I was never good enough. She'd harp on me about how I wasn't readin' with 'real' emotion; that I had lost my 'freshness,' that I wasn't the same person anymore.

43

"She even said," Jennifer was shaking her head in what appeared to be disbelief and with accumulated exhaustion and frustration, "I was 'cheating—cheating the dead, cheating the memory of the dead.' That's when she really tried to make me feel guilty by sayin' they deserved more than that—that I jus' didn't have any respect for 'em. Sometimes she'd get ugly and say, 'You probably don't have any feelings for your dead mother, or how else how could you be so callous?'

"Well, nothin' was changin', except I started hatin' the puppet show." She sighed and began to fidget. "I kept gettin' more nervous. It jus' wasn't fun for me. Joan, I think, she began to realize I didn't want to continue, but I jus' wasn't talkin' about it. Things, the tension, began to get heavy, really heavy at home between us."

I could see Jennifer's lips pressing together as she momentarily gathered her thoughts. Sitting on the edge of the bed, her posture shifted—she was rigid and straight-backed, but she hitched herself to the very edge of the bed and the muscles in her thighs were taut from the additional weight put on them. She looked as if she were about to bolt from where she sat.

"And so, I began to hate gettin' out'a bed and goin' to breakfast, 'cause Joan would always end up talkin' about the previous night, goin' over my performance (she even made notes). It got really bad and strange near the end, when she started talkin' about how rotten I must feel about lettin' her down, disappointin' her with my performance. That's what she called it: *my* performance.

"It was about that time when she started talkin' about suicide, askin' me if I had ever felt like committin' suicide. First, she'd go over my mother dyin' and how I must have felt. Then, how awful my life with my father was on the ranch, havin' to suddenly leave college 'cause I got pregnant. She'd say she understood how I would feel suicidal under the strain of these circumstances.

"That was the past. So then . . . she would start talkin' about the present. It was always about me lettin' her down, not doin' my best. She'd say 'I know you feel awful. I know, though, you're trying to do your best.' But she'd always end up sayin', 'Now, don't feel that way. I don't want you to get suicidal on me. I know you are trying, but you just seem to be sinking deeper into depression. You'll get better—I hope.'

"Near the end," Jennifer's shoulders drooped and she seemed to pull into herself, "she'd tell me how she could see I was depressed and she was really worried. She could tell that look: the same one her two other lovers had just before they killed themselves. She'd actually say, 'Please, please, don't do it. I just can't take it anymore. I don't know what I'd do if . . . oh God—not again!'

"It was really crazy," said Jennifer, "'cause she'd reach over and hug me, but it didn't feel warm and carin', like when you love someone. It felt . . . it felt strange: her body was hard and tense, like she was holdin' back her true feelin's. The look in her eyes wasn't nice. It was more like her body: so . . . hard and tense. You know,"

Jennifer shuddered as if a cold chill had run through her, "sometimes I'd have an image of Joan pushin' me over a cliff."

"A very powerful image, Jennifer, as if you are feeling—"

Before I could finish my sentence, there was a bright flash from the window that illuminated the already-lit room, followed by a *clap!* and a heavy roll of thunder. Shocked by the sudden flash and noise, we looked at the window as it rattled. Having been so absorbed in the session, we had been oblivious to the rain outside. Now the rain was coming down hard and the wind was blowing in gusts. The window held, but it sounded like it was taking a beating.

Trying to bring my attention back to Jennifer, I said, "That last statement of yours was very powerful and seems to hold a lot of meaning for you. Maybe we can pick up on it in our next session."

"O.K.," Jennifer said, distracted by both the force and ferocity of the storm and the one thing that seemed to provide both a view of its power and a fragile protection against it: the window. She got up and walked over to the window. She stood there, continuing to watch the sheets of water flow down the glass. I wondered at her fascination, whether she was distracted by the window itself, or by what she saw through it. At that moment, I thought about the symbolism of the window as a possible metaphor for the ego, struggling to hold at bay the psychic forces raging against it.

"You think it's gonna hold?" I asked ironically, hoping that my exaggerated, wide-eyed look, mimicking an actor in an old silent flick, would communicate a sense of humor to my question.

My attempt at a bit of humor got a response from Jennifer. She shook her head in mock disbelief, mirroring my attempt to engage her, then raised her eyebrows as if to say "Who knows?"

"It's O.K. I know where there's a piece of plastic," she said, playing along with our little skit, the corners of her mouth turning upward with obvious amusement.

I looked at my watch and said, "I think it's time we wrapped up for tonight."

Jennifer looked almost relieved by my suggestion and nodded. "When will I see you next?"

"How about Wednesday? I'm out of town Thursday and Friday. If there's a serious reason you need to speak to someone, I'll have a back-up at the clinic. The only thing is, you'll need to go in and see the clinician there. But first, make sure there's availability. Usually, they can squeeze a person in—especially someone who's an existing patient."

Given her displacement and emotional turmoil, I felt it prudent and therapeutic to make the arrangements to see her Wednesday and to have backup support at the clinic if she needed it.

"All right, I understand. But I think I'll wait for you," she said timidly.

"It's just a backup, Jennifer, if you need it. That's all," I said.

"I'll be here. You know, I've started working. Bernard gave me a job. So I'm gonna be here."

This time, contrary to my previous misgivings, I felt she would be safe at the hospice and she would be there this coming Wednesday. But, I reminded myself I had been wrong about patients before, so I tried to remind myself to call first. "Well, I'll see you Wednesday. Goodnight."

In my room that night, I found myself preoccupied with the session with Jennifer: the emotional intensity, the strange history of the young woman, and the lack of closure that the process of documentation and review of my case notes usually brought me. I read something entertaining, but remained agitated. Looking above my desk and gazing at a painting that had been in my family for generations usually gave me a vicarious escape. The jagged, snow-capped mountain could be seen from the perspective of a leafy, green canopy of old oaks, and a trail led down to a serene lake. This time, though, it triggered something else, something Jennifer had said: *Your eyes are green.* I could hear Jennifer's voice saying, *the same color as Joan's were.*

Green. Green—I realized what had been troubling me. Transference. My green eyes. Yes! An all-too-familiar occurrence in the therapeutic process: the upset patient transfers her personal experience onto the therapist.

Therapist Notes: Lacking insight, she, Jennifer, associating my green eyes with Joan's, inhibited the process of gathering the necessary therapeutic information—trying to determine Jennifer's risk of suicide, i.e., lethality. My inquiry provoked suspicion because of the patient's initial association of the color of my eyes with Joan's eyes, her ex-lover. Furthermore, my inquiry into her own possible suicidal ideation and intention aroused in the patient suspicion that my motives and Joan's were the same, i.e., to manipulate her to commit suicide. Previous diagnosis of depression with anxious mood is exacerbated by symptoms of paranoia.

After I closed the patient's file, I climbed into bed and listened to the storm pounding on the windows and roof. The deluge gradually lessened. Finally, there was only the sound of water, dripping, a susurrus of wind along the eaves of the house, and a branch and its leaves scraping against the windowpane. The drip, drip, drip segued into the wet, dripping trees in the Bohemian Forest.

· · · · ·

There was a faint knock on his door, then again. Evan looked up behind him to see the door opening quietly. Finally, Ruth poking her head into his room. She whispered to him to get up, to go down to the lake for a swim before *Fruestueck,* breakfast. She hurried Evan along, told him to be quiet and not to alert the other girls. Ruth kept looking back down the hall as sentinel, to see if anyone had been roused.

It was drizzling as they walked down the muddy, dirt road with the dark, wet, dripping forest around them. The trees were set back about twenty feet on either side of them, where dense grass and small, colorful wildflowers bloomed. To their right, the forest had been cleared and a farmhouse stood up a sloping hill. Coming down the grade, two young men strode toward them. Each had a *Wanderstab,* a walking stick. One was blonde, his hair pulled back tightly into a small ponytail at his neck, the other brunette with wavy hair. The men were young, tall, and ruggedly handsome with a powerful, determined gait. Before they all met, the trail veered off and Ruth and Evan made the gradual descent to the hidden lake.

They stood at the water's edge. The lake was perfectly still, placid and grey. The mist hung above the surface of the water and all but obscured the trees of the forest—trunks and limbs outlined as wavering, ephemeral apparitions here, there, and then lost, replaced by others in the spectral dance. With fine drizzle falling on them, Ruth began to undress. She slipped off her boots and used them as the only dry place for her clothes. Unbuttoning her pants, she pulled pants and underwear off in one quick motion and placed them carefully off the ground. She straightened up, looked over at Evan, and slowly pulled her heavy sweater up over her head, her breasts slipping out to rest against her chest. Ruth stood majestic, long-legged, with her sculpted torso, her long auburn hair falling in folds over her sloping, white shoulders. She noticed that he noticed. She walked over to the lake and waded into the water, not looking backward. With the water halfway up to her waist, she heard the splash of Evan next to her and she dipped down into the water, keeping her head above the surface; her hair glistening with tiny, silver droplets. They gazed ahead, the two of them moving in silence toward the middle of the lake.

The water was cold. There was only the sound of them taking in air as their hands and arms made small tight circles, pulling them toward the center of the lake;

occasionally the sound and rhythm of their breath was broken by the underwater paddle of their feet breaking the surface of the water. A rock began to emerge as they swam closer to the dark grey presence. It was only partially visible, raising a foot or two out of the water with its smooth, wet surface. The rock was large enough for them to pull themselves halfway out of the water to rest on the rounded, slightly conical head of what was a very large, submerged mass.

Ruth, partly kicking and partly pulling herself upward, then lay on the rock, breathing hard, fighting the cold. Evan slid up and balanced himself next to her, panting in short, almost spasmodic breaths. Ruth slowly turned herself over and lay on her back, bracing her body with her hands against the slippery mound and gazing into the grey void. Finally resting her cheek against the slick, hard surface, she looked unabashedly into his eyes.

He watched as she languidly closed her eyes and brought her head back into profile, her breathing adjusting itself to the lack of exertion, her chest rising and falling rhythmically. Then, slowly she let herself slide down and slip partially into the water, raising the shimmering grey surface of the water up to her navel, then to the edge of her ribcage; sinking a little lower. It was her glistening thighs and breasts that helped to keep her afloat. The whiteness of her breasts and pink tight nipples contrasted vividly against the dark grey water and the still lighter grey fog around and above her. As if in a dream, the image disappeared as she slowly began to glide off of the rock and into the water again. They swam back to the shore together, not touching, not looking at one another, but very aware of themselves and of each other.

Evan and Ruth dressed in silence, neither making an attempt to look at the other. They walked hurriedly, the sound of their boots sucking against the clinging mud. Ruth said they would need to get back before everyone was in the dining hall, and began to run—tried to run, *suck-plop-suck-plop*. Motioning for Evan to hold back as they neared the chalet, she called back to him to come and watch the eventide on the rock outcropping below the playing turf. *"Kommst du ja?* You'll come, yes?"

Evan watched as Ruth reached the porch, pulled off her muddy boots, then rushed through the door and up the stairs. He waited a few minutes before he went into the chalet to join the group for breakfast. He sat next to Ilse, a short, plump blonde with merry, light brown eyes, full of fun. The banter had begun; the games were next.

CHAPTER FOUR

Wednesday, February 8

By Wednesday, the last of the storms had passed, and the drive over to the hospice was easy and uneventful. This time, even though I felt relatively certain about Jennifer's "I'll be here," I called in advance. Bernard said in his usual laconic style that "Jenny" was there. He then volunteered that he'd offered Jennifer a job and she had taken it.

Although there was no rain or flooded streets, now there was the wind. If the gusts were really bad, a lot of trees would be brought down around town. Last year, hundreds of old eucalyptus were dislodged, littering the parks with their forlorn trunks, branches, and upturned roots.

Tonight, the constant sound of hissing wind was like that of an angry cat or a snake, ready to strike. Unlike the previous nights with the even drumming of the rain and occasional blasts of wind, strong, random and unpredictable gusts shook the already loosened window violently. The scratching of the rats behind the walls went unnoticed.

"Those experiences with Joan seem to have left you feeling very alone and vulnerable," I said. "Also, I haven't heard you speak of any of her friends or social circle."

"She didn't have any," Jennifer replied.

"None? None at all?" I inquired.

"No. It was just me and her, and that's the way she wanted it. Nobody came over. We didn't even eat out, since she thought it was too expensive, or we could eat better at home, or we could have, as she'd say, 'quality time' together. She worked all day in her garage (that was the workshop) where she made all of the dolls and, I suppose, where she read and wrote the scripts for her 'shows'."

The resentment and suppressed anger Jennifer felt toward the puppets and the strange theatrical productions were apparent by the look of disdain that flashed across her face and the sarcasm in her voice when she used the words "her shows."

"She could stay in there for hours" said Jennifer. "Sometimes, she didn't even come out for lunch. She didn't need anyone—not even me, I guess." Jennifer tilted her head and breathed out, showing by the expression on her face recognition of the lack of respect Joan had for her. "Myself, I looked after the house, watched T.V., or read. That's about it."

I began to form a tentative diagnosis of Joan, trying to better understand Jennifer. But there were too many unanswered questions left in Jennifer's account and in Joan's absence to arrive at a credible assessment. As a result, I waited to hear more.

I wanted to offer Jennifer a way to reminisce. "Alone in the house with no one to talk with during the day, I think I would feel lonesome. I wonder if it reminded you of being on the ranch, growing up with only your dad and yourself?"

I knew self-disclosure, expressing my own personal feelings, even if they were framed hypothetically, was a bit risky—the timing may be premature. Therapy would either deepen for the patient or we'd have to re-establish the current level of trust.

"Well," Jennifer began haltingly, "I did feel lonesome there—*with* Joan! But I didn't have that kinda feelin' on the ranch. It was different. There was always somethin' that needed doin.' You never felt really bored. No time to.

"And I always had company," she said wistfully. "There was Buck, my horse. He was a beauty. His daddy was a thoroughbred. I'd ride the range, lookin' for strays, or me and Buck would just amble over to a little hill and watch the sunset together." I saw her face brighten. "We really have beautiful sunsets; the sunrise is beautiful, too. You'd have to see 'em. I really miss—"

I could see how deeply Jennifer felt at that moment about home, the open spaces, and the reverence she had for the land. I noticed that another thought had intruded for her and she was brought back to what she had been talking about earlier. A certain darkness and anxiety described her mood as she stared at me, transfixed by this earlier memory.

"You know, I started goin' through all her books—Joan's, since she was workin' during the day, and I found a lot of books on dolls and puppets." She paused, possibly waiting for some feedback from me.

"It sounds as if you were feeling curious about the books and wanted to know more about what she did and why."

Jennifer nodded slowly. "Uh-huh. That's true, but . . . but, it wasn't just the puppets, how to make 'em and all of that. It was," she squinted, her eyes narrowing, "it got deeper than that—the weird part— all the psych stuff in some of the books, how the puppets affected the audience and even the puppeteer, what kinds of emotions came up and why. She even had a few books on using puppets in therapy. She made notes in the margins about her parents, her uncle, and her last two lovers. All sorts of things."

I found myself wanting to know more about Joan's background and asked, "Did Joan go to college? It appears she had some very serious interests."

"Mmmm, she told me she studied psychology, then ceramics and the theater. I think she ended up with a degree in theater, where she was doin' makeup and makin' things for the actors like masks and costumes. Things like that.

"There were a lot of books on psychology and therapy, especially the kinda books you see on depression or fears, anger. I think you call 'em 'how-to' books. She wrote a lot of stuff in those books, too, all over some pages, sometimes sayin' 'use in script' or 'change word' to this or that."

I could see she was starting to get agitated. Her breathing was becoming shallower. She was opening and closing her hands. Her eyes darted back to the window furtively, like something or someone might be lurking about. I focused on her behavior and watched carefully, assessing for signs of paranoia or schizophrenia and the possible loss of contact with reality.

"Looks like you're feeling insecure about something."

Nodding her head in agreement, Jennifer said warily, "Yeah, the wind rattling the window makes me wonder if it's gonna hold. On the ranch, sometimes with really bad storms we'd have a window blow out—'cause of the wind—and the rain would come pourin' in. Usually, it was somethin' that got picked up and was carried right on through—like a branch. At least, there's no rain to worry about, t'night.

"Anyway," she straightened up and looked intently at me, "One evening, Joan got really angry at me. She kept sayin' I was stupid, that I should know all my lines by heart. She said I wasn't tryin' hard enough.

She said she'd been patient with me, but . . . I was just stupid; she'd been wrong about me. I couldn't even read the lines with the right emotion. I was just like all the rest of 'em.

"And she went on and on, but this was really awful. She said, 'Your father was right about you: you're no good. You just can't do anything right. Something's wrong with you.' She jus' kept goin' on and on. Finally, I couldn't take it anymore.

"I got so angry, I lost control. I told her she was weird, that the plays, the dolls were weird. I ran out of the room, into her studio, locked the door and told her I wasn't comin' out. She was yellin' at me at the top of her lungs, 'You come out right now! If you don't, then I'm calling the police on you! You have no right to be in there!' Then she started callin' me names and that's when I jus' let go.

"I threw something against the wall. I can't remember what—some kind of pot she made. Smashed it to pieces. She was screamin' even louder now, 'I hate you!

I hate you! You bitch, I hate you! I wish you'd die! Die! Die! Like the rest of those no-goods! Like your worthless, rotten mother!'

"When she said that about my mother, I guess I really lost my head, 'cause I started throwin' and smashin' all kinds of things.

"By this time she was cryin' and beggin' me to come out. That's when I started goin' through the drawers in her workroom. I don't know what I was lookin' for, but I couldn't help myself. Then—

"And, I . . . I—," her rigid posture on the bed collapsed and she folded over. Her elbows dropped to her knees, and Jennifer covered her face with her hands, sobbing.

"In her drawer, I found . . . I found this!" She jumped up and pulled her suitcase from under the bed, flung it open, dug deeply, then twisted around to face me with her outstretched hand, tears flowing down her cheeks. She gasped, "I found *me,* look!" She was holding a doll's head that looked remarkably like her own and thrust it into my hand.

When she saw my shocked expression, she reached back into the suitcase as I examined the doll's head, noticing the fine workmanship that had captured the likeness of the young woman who stood before me. As I looked up, she handed me a headless doll with a sleeveless shirt, then pulled out the torn fabric of what was left of the original shirt with one hand.

"That's mine—my shirt!"

With her other hand, she thrust a photograph into my hand. I stared at a photograph of Jennifer, wearing the same shirt. I heard her say, "See? See it?" and I looked up.

Jennifer swiveled, reached into her suitcase, and turned back to face me, her hand trembling, "I didn't know she'd saved it. This, this is *my* hair. She had me cut some of my hair 'cause she said it was too long. But, look—"and she fell back against the bed, sobbing, her body convulsed by the memory. "That's my hair. She knew what I was thinkin' about doin', and she wanted me to do it. She wanted me to kill myself!"

Jennifer's voice dropped to a faint whisper, "Can't you see? Can't you see it's my hair?"

"I think I do, Jennifer."

I wondered about the reality of her history. Having no access to Joan, but not detecting a psychotic disorder in Jennifer, I was left to ponder the extraordinary circumstances and experiences of this young woman, as well as the enormous pain that comes with so much loss.

Jennifer's tears quickly gave way to composure again. I suspected that years of living on a ranch with a hard man, her father, created a stoicism and a sense of shame about crying or being emotionally out of control.

Lifting herself to a sitting position, she implored, "Don't you understand?"

Spent and drained of emotion, she said, exhausted, "The next day my things were out on the street." Her shoulders drooped and her arms went limp. "Now, at least you know the whole story. There's nothin' more to tell."

"I think we have more to talk about, Jennifer. But first, I think you need some rest and some sleep. I'll give you a telephone call tomorrow before I leave."

"Yeah, you're right. I just need to rest. Thank you. I want you to know I really appreciate everything."

"I know you do. I appreciate you saying that."

Seeing I wasn't moving, she said, "Really, I'll be all right t'night."

"You've been through a lot. I'm glad you've worked something out with Bernard. It'll help. You've got a place to stay and, the guys need you.

"Well, I'll see you here, Monday, at six. But tomorrow, I'll phone you during the day before I leave. If you need to speak to someone else while I'm gone, call the facility and ask for the therapist who is substituting for me while I am away."

I left the room as quietly as I had come in and closed the door behind me. When I got home, I tried to busy myself with some paperwork, but my mind wandered. Not ready to go to bed, I went over to the corner of the room and sank into the old, familiar chair, letting my head nestle into the folds and contours of its well-worn leather. I thought about Grandpa, years earlier, sitting me on his lap, singing a ditty, "And the cow jumped over the moon, moon, moon" and, pleasantly, comfortably, I drifted off, half-awake, half-asleep, images of the *Waldhuette* fading in and out of my consciousness.

. . . . .

He went down the stairs of the lodge to the far end of the playing field, where the grass gradually banked down to their meeting place, the rocky outcropping. Ruth sat quietly and turned when she heard his shoe grind loose rock on rock. Evan slipped down beside her, bent forward and looked over the ledge to the ground far below. A few trees hugged the side of the cliff, allowing him to change his perspective. He was clearly on top of the highest summit in the area. Their view was unencumbered. The forest covering the low mountains stretched out before them.

The sun had set. It was late and a faint peach glow was on the horizon. Above them, the sky was cloudless and beginning to turn a dark blue. No stars yet shone. A pale grey mist arose, spreading across the valleys to the foot of the mountains. The glow became a dark tangerine above the sun's timeless descent, dissolving into the color of the violet, a delicate reddish purple.

"There is a 'magic' and a 'power'," are the words that Ruth whispered. She said softly that there was something very ancient, something very primeval and compelling that drew her—part of her—yet ultimately repelled and frightened her. As they sat together, Ruth began to confide her story to Evan.

Ruth gazed off into space, then continuing to speak in German, she said earnestly, "*Meine Grossmutter war Jude,* my grandmother was a Jew."

Ruth hesitated on this somber note, which gave Evan the time to absorb the impact and weight of her words, pregnant with meaning and power. Ruth told Evan that her grandfather, a young German aristocrat, was studying French literature in Brussels when he met her grandmother, Sara, who was a student at a music academy. They married in Berlin in 1913. Her mother, Sigrid, was born only one week before the end of the Great War. Two other girls were born after 1933—an inauspicious time. Hitler was in power.

Evan felt Ruth's shoulder against his. Ruth spoke of a family in turmoil. He listened carefully as her voice became darker with an underlying tone of foreboding and apprehension, which conjured up for Evan the passionate and tragic tone poem, "The Isle of the Dead." The mist crawled higher up the slopes of the mountains, slowly enveloping everything but the gently rounded peaks, creating small islands in the sky, one isolated from the other by the white and grey blanket of fog. A deep silence settled upon them. Evan gazed at the remote islands and imagined those dark days—the increasing isolation of the Jews in German society.

Sigrid, her mother, Ruth began hesitantly, had gone to stay temporarily with her paternal uncle at the family's lodge in a small town in the Black Forest, while the rest of the family had gone in stages—not to arouse suspicion—to Brussels. War broke out before Sigrid could join them, stranding her in Germany. Peering over her shoulder to see if anyone were there, Ruth's voice became hushed and confidential, suggesting to Evan that what she was telling him was a secret. Her mother's true identity was discovered in the closing months of the war. Sigrid and her uncle were arrested, beaten, and crammed onto a truck, headed for Dachau. On the road, the truck was strafed by an allied plane. The truck crashed into a ditch, giving the prisoners a chance to escape. Sigrid fled into the surrounding countryside, where she was rescued weeks later by the Americans. *"Aber . . . mein Onkel war getoetet!* But . . . my uncle was killed. A bullet from the fighter had found him—not Sigrid. She had given him her seat to help relieve the pain of the beating he received from the Gestapo."

The mist had slipped over the ledge, bringing a chill to the air. Ruth wrapped her arms around her bare legs and clasped her hands together tightly, then vigorously tried to rub warmth back into her legs. She inched over toward Evan, and he felt the touch of Ruth's leg against his. She began to speak, telling Evan it was only three years ago her family had been contacted by relatives in America. They found Sigrid after a long search. Sigrid's mother and sisters flew to Munich for a reunion. Sigrid's father had passed away two years earlier.

Ruth's voice quavered as she described the meeting of her mother and grandmother. Ruth saw her mother cry for the first time ever. Her grandmother wrapped her arms around Sigrid and said again and again, *"Oh, ma petite fille, mein*

Kind . . . ich habe dich gefunden . . . oh, my little girl, my child . . . I have found you."

Ruth's voice choked and she stopped speaking. Finally, repeating ever so softly her grandmother's words, Ruth murmured, *"Je t'aime . . . ich liebe dich . . . ich liebe dich,* I love you . . . I love you . . . I love you."

Evan could see now Ruth was trying to speak, but began to grope for words. Ruth was struggling to describe her mother's emotional rebirth: Sigrid would look at Ruth and her brother and cry out, *"Sie sind euer Blut . . . euer Blut!* They are your blood . . . your blood!" Her mother sobbed uncontrollably, *"Unsere Familie sind hier!* Our family is here!" Evan watched as Ruth closed her eyes, saying *"Mein Blut . . . Mein Blut . . ."*

It was during the reunion that Ruth heard the story of their escape. Evan listened as the pace and urgency of Ruth's voice increased. With the German invasion of Belgium, the family rushed to France. As France collapsed, they set out on foot for Spain. Once over the frontier, they embarked from Sevilla for America. Evan noticed at this point Ruth seemed to shrink back into herself, her shoulders slumped, and her head dropped forward. After the war, her relatives in America would learn of the concentration camps. None of Sara's family in Belgium survived. "*Alle . . . wurden getoeten*," Ruth, murmured, pausing. Then using English for the first time that evening, she said, so that she would be sure Evan understood the full meaning of her statement, "*All of them . . . all of them were killed.*"

It was dark by now. Evan could see Ruth was exhausted—but relieved—to have told him about her family and herself. She stood up and said she wanted to go back alone, but she would save a seat for him at the table. Evan waited in the night and felt the tension inside of him. Having deeply absorbed so much emotionally-charged history from Ruth, he lay back and looked up at the starry nighttime sky. Finally, he watched as the mist crept around his body and enshrouded him in a grey, impenetrable cocoon. He waited. He waited for the Earth to absorb from him, to take from him the *Sturm und Drang*, the storm and turmoil, and to give back and to replenish him with its silence and emptiness. That is what he needed now.

Tonight was the celebration. The girls had one long table in the dining hall of the lodge. Another table was filled with the men's soccer club, a rowdy bunch of working-class locals. Two women, sitting alone, were invited to join the girls. Heidi and Gisela turned out to be students from Switzerland on holiday. They sat across from Evan. Against the far wall the two young giants Ruth and Evan had seen on their walk to the lake that morning, sat quietly. They seemed to enjoy their beer and food, but their reserve suggested to the revelers that they had no desire to engage themselves with anyone else in the room. In spite of their aloofness, the girls called out repeatedly to them, trying— unsuccessfully—to entice them over to their table. The room, with its lit fireplace, created a warm, wonderfully cozy feeling— *gemuetlichkeit*—while the dense grey mist and dampness grew outside. The high-spirited young people with their steins of beer were in a festive mood.

Evan sat at one end of the table between Ruth and Ilse, and had a good view of the entire room. Ilse shouted out that Ruth was a pianist. Soon everyone from the two long tables clamored for her to play, banging their steins on the table. Ruth held back, then relented. She walked over to the piano, sat down and lifted the cover, pulled the bench up behind herself and adjusted it carefully. At that point, she "owned the stage."

Ruth placed her hands on the keyboard, leaned forward slightly, and began to play. *Liebestraum,* the Dream of Love, filled the room. Note by note, the boisterous crowd was stilled. More than one hundred years of music, the old romantic melody by Litzt that had filled the souls of generations of men and women, reached out and touched a collective chord, caressing them, taming the wild, energetic band. It enwrapped the young women in their own thoughts and dreams; ensnared the men in its soft, tender melody of romance and love. Almost no one heard the last note fade off.

Ruth could see Evan from over the piano and she looked directly into his eyes. His eyes were wide, filled with awareness of the moment and the emotion that stirred within him. The mist rising over the mountains and forest set the spirits free— old lovers melding in their ethereal dance; the *gemuetlichkeit*, the sentimentality, and the glowing bond of community and of love bound one to the other. She connected to Evan in this moment, saw him nod his head, his eyes half-closed, intoxicated by the music and the evening.

Now the room erupted into an enthusiastic ovation. She nodded to the guitarist at the men's table and turned back to the piano and started to play again. Quickly the clapping died down, when the first few chords struggled to break through the noise. The guitarist began to accompany her and the two of them started to sing: *"Du, Du, liegst mir im Herzen; Du, Du, liegst mir im Sinn . . . "* "You, you, love me with all your heart; You, you are in my thoughts..." an old song, sung by generations. The men slid their arms over their fellow's shoulders, the women linked arms and everyone swayed back and forth together as they sang the old verses. Their mutual trust and good feeling was come to life in the flame of the night of music and song.

Almost as quickly, the mood shifted when a chorus of voices rose to the notes of popular beer drinking songs, one after another. By this time, Ruth had come back to the table and ensconced herself between friends, singing along with everyone else, when the guitarist struck another note and his buddies began to sing. The women at Ruth's table stopped singing and just looked at one another uncomfortably. The two Swiss stood up from their seats and turned to go. Evan asked Heidi why they were leaving.

She said they didn't sing these songs in Switzerland. Evan was perplexed, until Heidi remarked that they were singing one of the old marching songs of WWII. Another song began when the two young men sitting by themselves stood up. One, the blonde one, his face red with fury, yelled angrily to the table of revelers in coarse German, "*Halt euer Maul*!! Shut up!!"

Then in even coarser German, he sneered, "Who wants to hear that shit?"

One of the men at the table, drunken and bleary-eyed, protested loudly and started to stand up, when he was yanked down to his seat by his buddies. The two giants, as everyone called them, stalked out of the room.

The guitarist and some of the men, evidently not to be intimidated now that the two giants had left, started to play another marching song. Ruth and her friends began to leave the room as a group. Evan could see Ruth was shaken and withdrawn into herself. He came up to her, but she shook her head and went quickly up the stairs with the rest of the women.

The party was over.

CHAPTER FIVE

February 12 - March 22

Therapist Notes: Jennifer now came to the clinic for counseling and was actually able to make small donations, which increased her self-esteem. The ensnaring matrix that bound her to Joan, like the fatal silk of the spider's web to its prey, loosened at its core. Joan and suicide and the bizarre situation she found herself in were becoming infrequent topics. For the most part, the next five weeks lacked much of the intensity of those early sessions, except for the session on March 22nd.

Wednesday, March 22

"You old hag!" Jennifer, looked a bit confused, staring at the empty chair, and turned to me to say: "Well, Joan wasn't old.

I mean, she was eight years older than me, that's all."

"Jennifer," I said—not disapprovingly, but keeping her focused, "don't worry about the details here. Just go with the flow. Just stay in the moment. We're trying to get to how you are feeling now—in the present moment. It's O.K. if details like those are off."

Jennifer took a breath and nodded. "Yeah, that's what I'm callin' *you:* you old, old hag!" Jennifer stopped. She looked at me and said, "What did you say we're doin'?"

"Well," I said, "in this exercise we are role-playing. We use the chairs as props to do it. The goal is to express your feelings openly and directly by staying in the present: I am feeling angry . . . I feel sad or happy and so forth, O.K.?"

Jennifer looked pensive, absorbing the information, then tried again.

"You—" she hesitated ambivalently, "This isn't easy. It doesn't seem very real. I mean, there's an empty chair I'm lookin' at. It isn't—" She paused, pressed her lips together, then pushed her hair away from her face impatiently. "You old hag," she repeated. "Yeah, that's what I'm callin' *you*: you old, old hag.

"You were older. I mean—" Jennifer stammered and paused, catching herself using the past tense in her sentence. "You should know what you're doin' to me. You're a witch. Yeah, that's what you are: a cold, mean old witch!

"I trusted you. I felt—" Jennifer stopped again, frustrated with herself. Then she turned to look at me. "That was the past, wasn't it?" She looked discouraged and dropped her eyes to the floor.

"Jennifer, just go with the flow," I said again. "Sometimes you'll slip back to the past, but that's what happens to all of us daily; it's not unusual. I'm glad you're catching yourself during this exercise. If I think it's really important to stop you, then I will, O.K.?

"Remember, I am *not* Joan. Would you continue, please? I feel—"

That seemed to reassure her. The muscles in her face relaxed. She turned back to face the empty chair with what appeared to be conviction. "I feel . . . I feel let down, kinda sad inside. You were like a mother to me or an older sister. At first, you held me close and were kind and caring. Now, you're cold. Do you hear me? Cold. I feel alone. I need to be held and told that you . . . that someone wants—" Jennifer hesitated, and the longer she hesitated, the more she felt unable to continue.

"Jennifer, would you go over to the empty chair and sit there, please?" She took the seat, obviously feeling awkward, and looked at me. I saw the uncertainty in her eyes, but I also knew she had come to trust me and to trust what we were doing in therapy.

"Now, as you sometimes say to me, 'This is strange.' Well, this next part of the exercise may seem just that way, a little strange. I would like you to pretend to be

Joan. You're sitting in Joan's chair. Imagine, if you will, what Joan now would say to you in response to your accusation that she is cold and doesn't hold you, nor is she kind to you anymore."

Jennifer sat there looking at me, wondering to herself, I suspected, what the heck was going on.

"Will you please give it a shot, Jennifer?"

"You . . . Jennifer," she fumbled for the words, "you don't deserve my . . . my love." Jennifer's voice dropped to a whisper with these last few words.

"Jennifer, would Joan say that the way you just said it—in a whisper?" I watched carefully to see her reaction to my question, hoping to avoid the negativity she associated with Joan's critiques or her plays.

Jennifer, peering at the empty chair where she had been sitting, straightened her back, the muscles of her face constricting into a mask of hard, unyielding emotion. She said severely, "Jennifer, you do *not* deserve my love. You are a bad girl. I have tried, you know—if you are honest with yourself—to be like the mother you lost and never had when you really needed her most, but—" Her lips pursed into a narrow, prim, straight line. "You don't . . . you do *not* even know what love is."

I saw the transformation occur before me: Joan, in all of her punishing severity, with all of her conditions for love, was figuratively here. Leaning forward, I gestured to the empty chair. "Jennifer, if you will now take your old seat, this time you have the opportunity to respond to what Joan just said to you."

Jennifer moved back to her original chair with no visible resistance and with increasing confidence, gaining a sense of the basics of the exercise, she now appeared ready for her riposte; she seemed ready to have herself reply to Joan and, I thought, possibly to deal with her anger directly.

"No!" Jennifer said determinedly. "I am feeling pissed off. You're not doin' that to me. You're *not* makin' it my fault again! You knew exactly what you were—I mean—are doin.' It was all an act. I see that now. I'm like one of your dolls to you. Just another one of your freaky dolls. You want to turn me into one of 'em. Then, it won't be long, will it? Will it, you witch?!"

She began to answer her own question sarcastically. "Then, I'll be dead! Jus' like Rebecca and Janice. But that won't stop you. You'll move on to someone else and kill them, too, you evil old thing!" Jennifer leaned forward, her anger growing, "You pretending to be my mom, what a joke, a sick, mean joke! You all sweet and stuff at first," she said, scorn etching each of her words, "finding out all you need to know about Mother, then turning it on me—like a snake!

"Remember, in the beginning, you wanted to know exactly how Mother talked to me—the words she used? What she cooked? Even how she held me? Everything." Jennifer's voice was audibly softening. It became almost plaintive and communicated a deep sense of pain. The suffering spread across the features of her face. "You violated everything sacred to me.

"Yeah . . . *violated.*" Jennifer said the word almost as if she were becoming aware of the word and its meaning for the first time. It also touched some raw and primitive feeling within her. Her face contorted into a fierce expression, her teeth bared in a reflexive show of rage. Then she screamed, "You bitch! I hate you! You rotten bitch!!" Jennifer's fists clenched and the veins in her neck bulged.

Nodding my head vigorously, my voice rising angrily, I clearly affirmed Jennifer's feelings. "You're sounding like you are feeling *really* angry with Joan. *Really* angry!" I growled.

"I am!" Then, astonished with herself, with her behavior, "I am," she said, sounding more subdued and looking almost apologetic—apologetic for her angry outburst.

"Yeah, you sound like you're angry, but maybe also a little embarrassed or ashamed to be showing it; kind of like you're out of control."

"Uh huh. I'm feelin'—" She went silent. I could see it was difficult for Jennifer to acknowledge, let alone use the *word* for what she was feeling.

"Well, Jennifer, it's O.K. to be angry here. I can see it really pushed all your buttons when you heard Joan talk about love. Didn't she say, "You don't know . . . what was it? You don't know—" I said, encouraging her to pick up the dialogue.

"You don't know what love is," said Jennifer disgustedly, slowly finishing the sentence verbatim.

"Well, I think right now you're looking at me, Jennifer, but I have a sense you really have something more to say to Joan, and—"

She broke into my sentence, turned back to the empty chair, and started to speak to Joan directly, without censor.

"Joan . . . *you* don't know what it is. Love. No! No, you don't!

"You said you love me and cared, and that would never change. You said a woman's love was pure—not like a man's, who just wants sex and uses a woman for his own pleasure. But," Jennifer's face contorted again with anger, mixed with disdain, "but you . . . that's what you did! You threw me away when you were done with me. Todd, my own husband, didn't even treat me like that. He tried; he tried hard to do the right thing, but *you*—" she trailed off, silent again.

"Jennifer, please shift your focus to the present time," I said softly. "You're doing very well."

"You're treatin' me like that, like some *thing* you use. You're callin' it love, but it isn't. My mother loved me. I know that. You're like . . . I mean, you look like my mother: her long, dark hair." Jennifer slightly closed her eyes, remembering. "Her skin was soft and smooth. But your eyes—no, not your eyes—they are *not* the same, yours are green, jus' like the cat's.

"I don't feel safe with you. I felt safe with Mother." Jennifer sighed. "Mother's eyes were . . . Mother's were kind. They were almost blue with grey in 'em that—" Jennifer caught herself reminiscing, came back to the present moment, and said sharply, "You got cat eyes. You play with me jus' like the cat does with a bird, before it kills it." Shaking her head slowly and closing her eyes, almost in disbelief of what had happened to her, she said, "That's the kinda animal you are: cruel and . . . sadistic!"

Jennifer began slowly, "I know why you're so hateful." Jennifer's voice had a cutting, biting edge to it. Her gaze was unwavering, fixed as if ready to strike a deadly blow to a rattlesnake. "You don't wanna talk about it, but—" Jennifer held back momentarily, "it's because . . . of what your uncle *did* to you. He bedded—no, uh, uh—he . . . *screwed* you. He didn't want you. He didn't love you or care about you. He just took what you had and used you like one of your toys—like one of your crazy dolls."

I was aware that Jennifer thought deeply and long about her experiences and her sessions. She had drawn her own conclusions and also was expressing herself naturally, without self-censoring her legitimate thoughts and feelings, especially her anger.

Jennifer continued to excoriate Joan. "So . . . where was your aunt? Where was she? She had to know. Yes. She did know." The realization of what she said only increased the growing bitterness in Jennifer. "I remember you said she hit you when you told her. She *knew* what was going on. But . . . nothin'! She did nothin'— nothin' to protect you. So you hate everyone. You want all of us to pay and to die. Jus' so you can go on livin' and destroyin' everyone around you. Makin' your stupid dolls. Pretendin'. Tryin' to get rid of your shit!

"It was only one big show to you." Jennifer caught her breath and said, exasperated, "Nothin', no one else mattered to you," shaking her head slowly, "no one, no one at all," and her voice trailed off into resignation. The expression on her face all the while said only this: loathing.

"Maybe, Joan would like to say something—to make you understand, to have her say," I said, dispassionately.

"I think I'm tired of this." Then suddenly, Jennifer reacted as if a bolt of lightning had struck her. "What? *What* did you jus' say? That makes me feel—" Jennifer hesitated. She glared at me, unable to speak.

"Angry? So . . . you are feeling angry?" I said strongly, glaring back at her.

"Yeah. Yeah. About Joan, about Joan wantin' to have *her* say. What do you think she was doin' all those months?" Jennifer said indignantly.

I heard the anger behind her words again and, I watched Jennifer—without prompting—and she stood up from her chair and sat in Joan's chair.

Now I tried to capture Jennifer's outrage and the intensity of her personal violation and betrayal. "I think you said to

Joan, 'it was all a big show . . . no one else mattered.'"

Still furious with Joan, it was a struggle for Jennifer to assume an empathetic role.

"Well, at this moment—" I said, my voice and expression appearing as if I were thinking aloud, "I doubt," I paused, "Joan would be sitting the way you are. You look as if you are ready to spring right at her. Joan probably would be sitting—" I sat up straight in my chair.

I saw the change—Jennifer adjusted her posture to the prim, straight-backed disciplinarian. Now the muscular, internal kinesthetic reality began to translate itself emotionally into the thinking, the feeling and behavior of her character. "It was all a big show," I recollected, prompting her to action.

"Jennifer, Jennifer," she sighed disapprovingly, "this is just like you. Emotional when you shouldn't be, and *no* emotion when you should be expressing it. Just none, none at all." She lifted her hands and arms and expanded them outwardly, slowly in what should have been a grand, theatrical gesture—mimicking a flower opening, but the gesture was constricted, the fingers crooked like the talons of a bird of prey, the arms squeezed tightly against her ribcage. "Express your emotions . . . freely . . . naturally."

She smirked, and shook her head dismissively. "You're just emotionally retarded, dear. A retard. That, that is your problem." Now, hissing as she sucked in her breath, "I just couldn't count on you when I needed you most. I could have loved you if only you could have been there for me, too. But you were out of touch with your own feelings. Just too much into yourself, too self-involved. Just too self-absorbed." Shaking her head again and closing her eyes to show her utter exasperation with Jennifer and all she tried to do to help her, she took a deep breath and finally said, "Why should I have expected *you* could be any more than some silly cowgirl from the country?"

As Jennifer really began to identify with the role of Joan, she shrugged her shoulders, clucking her disapproval as a young mother is wont to do with her unruly toddler. "Dear, you're just no good in your performances, just no good in the shows." Jennifer sat there rigid and hard, as if she were frozen in time. She looked almost catatonic until I saw her blink and her eyes flash. I could see she was furious. She was ready to reengage Joan.

Without saying a word, I gestured for her to retake her chair, her *own* chair, which she saw out of the corner of her eye. Turning to me momentarily, I saw the anger turned to fury in her gaze. I gestured again, wordlessly. Jennifer moved over.

"Your shows! I am *disgusted* with you! Your stupid shows. You bitch, all you can think about are your shows! I see you for who you are—you pathetic, crazy, old witch!

"I'm glad you're out'a my life . . . for good!

"I never want to see you again!

"I never want to hear from you . . . again!

"Goodbye!!"

Jennifer started to stand up, but stopped midway and slowly retook her seat. She was still seething with unexpressed anger and resentment. Fulminating, she said sarcastically, "The sex. You even ruined that!

"Tenderness, just simple tenderness. Where did it go?" she said imploringly. "I jus' feel empty."

The sudden tempering of her anger toward Joan when she recalled those early tender experiences in their relationship, changed abruptly when she realized where she was. "You squeeze everything out of lovemakin'. You make it into something else. You always have to be in control. You hover over me like some old sow and squeeze me like a vise. I can hardly breathe—you layin' on me like a big sack of flour, suffocatin' me. I am just . . . there, and you do what you want to do. It never changes. Even here, you are givin' directions, tellin' me about what you want. You never ask me what I want. You're . . . I'm so . . . angry."

Jennifer took a moment to think. "You're just a selfish bitch!

"I can see now that's how your uncle must have treated you. He was on top—top dog! He jus' took what he wanted." Jennifer said, disgusted, "Yeah, that's right. You were jus' a doll he put up on the shelf when he was through with you, and then brought you down again when he wanted to screw you.

"I am," her voice suddenly becoming sympathetic, "I am truly sorry for you—" Jennifer caught herself, saying how she felt. "I feel sorry for you. I do, but—"

"But what, Jennifer?" I said, seeing if she would complete her train of thought. I watched Jennifer as her jaw set, determined to finish what she had to say.

She said, gripping the arms of the chair, "You have no right, no fuckin' right to do this to me!

"I loved you," she said angrily. "I really
. . . loved you," she said again, the tone of
her voice only barely softening. "I trusted
you," and she paused. Evidently those
words "I trusted you" brought back the
intensity of Jennifer's anger and her deep
sense of betrayal.

I saw Jennifer's eyes narrow as she
appeared to consciously control and
contain her body's response to the sense of
outrage she was feeling.

"Yes, I loved you. But now, now I feel
nothin'. I feel nothin' for you at all!" shouted
Jennifer, and she stood up defiantly.
"I don't love you, anymore! I don't want to
love you, anymore! Nothin'!!"

Jennifer was enraged. "It's over! It's
over for me, Joan. Goodbye!"

I could see Jennifer looked spent and
drained, emotionally exhausted; but it was
a positive exhaustion, one of relief. It was
as if she had run a marathon and just
crossed the finish line. There was only the
sound of Jennifer's breathing, slowly

returning to normal. I did not move or say anything.

She nodded and, acknowledging her exhaustion, she declared, "I'm done for this evening. I'm really tired." She paused, then said, "I jus' need to collect myself."

It wasn't long before she looked over at me and smiled slightly, clasping her hands together in front of herself. "I never imagined all that was inside of me. Never."

"Jennifer, I get the sense you've gotten a lot off of your chest. You've worked hard to get here," I said, looking into her eyes.

"Yeah, I guess I did." She nodded her head in agreement. Moments later, I saw her taking mental stock of her experience and reflecting over the event in some disbelief.

"I think . . . no, I know . . . I'm finished, really finished for t'night."

"You're welcome to sit down if you would like."

"No thanks. I'm ready."

"Well, I'll see you at the same time, same place next week."

"O.K. Same time, same place—next week," she said.

That same night, I mulled over my notes, thinking about Jennifer, where she had come from and where she had arrived, so to speak. It was an emotional—even a dramatic—session in the room.

Therapist Notes: This session did appear to crystallize her anger and her resentment toward Joan. The session provided an opportunity for Jennifer consciously to give herself permission to express her pent-up anger and rage in a positive and constructive manner. She appeared to come to grips with much of the trauma and turmoil of the past months. She not only has a better understanding of herself generally, but she has developed some new coping skills as well. It remains to be seen how her feelings about her relationship with a woman—with Joan—will be resolved:

whether she will reengage with another woman or choose to return to a heterosexual relationship with a man. Note: work on assertion training with her in our coming sessions.

. . . . .

Evan awoke sleepily to the words, "*Es ist kalt zu mir.*" He heard again "*Es ist kalt zu mir,* I'm cold," and he became aware of the soft intonation of Ruth's voice, whispering to him in the more lyrical Bavarian dialect. Immediately, he felt the warmth of her body next to his under the blanket. The moon had risen and the light shone through the small window, illuminating the room. He reached across his body to feel her hair spread in undulating waves; it overflowed and covered the pillow. He pressed his nose deeply into the wavy texture of her hair, and its perfume filled him with desire. He sensed her growing passion by the way she pressed her face close to his chest and almost imperceptibly inhaled the smell and musk of his body. His senses were alert and his pulse quickened. She pulled back the cover and then moved on top of him, straddling his hips.

"Oh weh, It's painful!" and she pulled back.

He realized she had frozen up, her muscles tightening uncontrollably. Pulling her back to him and to his side, he lay across from her and spoke gently in English. He wanted her to separate herself from Germany and this night of the old marching songs.

"Everything is O.K." and he kissed her lightly on the lips, "O.K." He kissed her on her forehead lightly, again and again. "Tonight, you are here with me and we are safe, safe." Seeing she was beginning to relax and further become supple, he continued to whisper reassuringly in English. Finally, feeling her response, he said in German softly, *"Es ist schon gut,* It's O.K. *Du bist sicher, sicher.* You're safe, safe.

"Ich bin Amerikaner, I'm an American. *Sehst du,* do you see?" and he took her hand and placed it on himself, reminding her of when they were in the shower. He

was different—not German. *Bescheidet*. He reached up and caressed her brow. He drew closer and traced the line of her lips with his fingertip. He felt the corners of her mouth turning up into a smile. He sensed she was aware of the reality of his presence and of his words, and she yielded. Slowly the fear dissolved and he pressed carefully against her, urging her gently so that she opened, and finally he sank deeply into her.

Late that night, Evan woke up from the movement of Ruth's body next to his. Ruth, asleep, was twisted up in the blanket and fighting to get disentangled. Her breathing was shallow, her head turned from side to side painfully; she whimpered and mewed and fought against some imaginary force in her dream. Evan called to Ruth. He did not touch her; he called over and again to her repeatedly. She opened her eyes but could feel nothing but the terror of her nightmare. She began to see the moonlit room and heard his voice calling to her gently.

Soon she began to quiet and lay still. Evan reached out to her and helped her disentangle herself. Afterward, when she lay there naked, sweating, she reached out and drew herself toward him. It was she who kissed him deeply, longingly. He responded. He would let her fight out her demons tonight. At first, he did not try to control or to dominate her. He was not insistent, but he was there. She exerted her own strength to overcome and to have power. Once fully aroused, he became passionate, matching her need. The ebb and flow reached a climax and there was a melding for them both. He was there many times for her that night, until she exhausted herself and him. Finally, sleep came in the early hours of dawn.

There was a firm knock on the door. When Evan opened his eyes and looked over, Ruth was gone. He inched his way over to the door, since the mattress was so close to it and reached up, lifted the latch and pulled the door open, covering himself with his blanket. He must have looked surprised and shocked, because Heidi— just outside his door—started laughing "*Grueetzi!* Greetings," she said heartily in Swiss German. One of the Swiss girls at his table from last night's party, Heidi offered to give him a ride back to Switzerland if he wanted. The soccer team left earlier that morning and the young woman named Ruth asked Heidi and Gisela if they would give him a lift out of the mountains—or he would be stranded there without a car.

As he was dressing, he was thinking about Ruth, the sex, the passion and . . . the fear. He wondered what she would do— if she really would go to the States. Ruth said since her own conversion to Judaism last summer, she wanted to be close to her extended family in California. She wanted to be away from home and Germany. Would she do it? At that moment, he heard Heidi call through the door, *"Kommst du?* Are you coming?"* He hoisted his backpack over his shoulder and looked one last time at the small window, imagining the light of the moon streaming through onto the pillow, Ruth's hair cascading over the white linen.

"Bitte, wir muessen gehen," urged Heidi, "Please, we must go."

With that, Evan walked out of the Forest Hut and to their car.

CHAPTER SIX

March 28 – May 23

Therapist Notes: There had been one death at the hospice—the death of the young man, Gary, blind and bedridden. The experience brought back memories for Jennifer of nursing her own mother, with cancer at home when she was a young teen. The experience of loss—then and now— left her feeling emotionally empty. Bernard, busy and brusque as he was, had, as Jennifer said, "been there" for her and let her grieve. She said that at one point Bernard reminded her of the living who still needed her help, so she picked herself up and got on with her job.

Jennifer was working at the hospice for room, board and a small stipend. Since taking on more responsibility, first as a housekeeper and part of the kitchen staff, and then as a direct caregiver to the residents, the regimen and purpose contributed to an overall improvement of her attitude and state of mind. She began to verbalize about future plans—nothing very solid or concrete, but very tentative goals nonetheless.

Wednesday, May 30

That afternoon after arriving at the clinic, I reviewed the caseload and read a sticker attached to the bottom of the sheet: *See front desk for letter regarding six o'clock appointment.*

The letter was dropped off by a young woman earlier today. She didn't say anything, except it was important you get the letter," said the volunteer at the desk, handing me the white envelope.

I opened the letter. Written in pencil on paper I recognized, the letter began:

Thank you very much for all you've done for me, but I'm leaving the hospice. I've got a job and a place to stay. I'm much better.

Thank you,
[signed] Jennifer

P.S.   I just couldn't say goodbye. I hope you understand.

I then called the hospice and Bernard answered.

"This is Evan. I've been talking with Jennifer. I have a note written by her."

Bernard remained silent. After a long pause, I heard him respond. "Uh-huh?"

"Uh-huh," I reflected ironically.

"She's gone," he said dryly.

Then, clearing his throat after an extended silence, Bernard said, "Hated to see her go. Jenny helped a lot. The guys really liked her. Think she's gonna be O.K. Lined up a job and a place to stay with a nice family."

Again, silence. Finally, he said, "What else can I say?"

"Thanks Bernard, for taking her in. It really made a difference. You were a real lifesaver."

"I wish I could be a lifesaver for the guys here," he said wearily.

"I know that they all appreciate you. I certainly do as well, Bernard," I confided. "Thanks again."

I hung up the phone several seconds after there was only the sound of the dial tone. I put Jennifer's letter back in the envelope and slipped it into my briefcase, walking into the tiny room I called my office. I sat there, feeling a loss, a loss of relationship, especially because I had not had the opportunity to bring some form of closure to it.

I thought, "This is more the norm than the exception here. I wish her well."

I got up and walked out to see if I had another patient.

CHAPTER SEVEN

One Year Later

Wednesday, May 22

When I came into the clinic, I went to the desk as usual and looked down at the roster. One name—my first patient—looked familiar. I turned around to see in the lobby a well-groomed young woman in a pantsuit, with a scarf and short leather jacket. Her blonde hair was cut just above her shoulders.

It was Jennifer. I readjusted my recollection of her in sessions during stormy nights at the hospice to the young woman sitting before me on this sunny, spring day.

I was genuinely surprised. She caught my eye as I went over and reached out my hand. "Hello, hello," I said. "What an unexpected surprise."

Nodding toward my "office," I said, "Please, come in. You may remember," I smiled wryly, "my office is still that same posh Beverly Hills suite."

I sat across from someone I now only vaguely recognized. Gone was the rancher's daughter in blue jeans and, instead, sitting in her place was a svelte, attractive young woman, composed, almost stylish. The lack of makeup (but for lipstick) brought back to me the Jennifer of old, who exuded a natural, outdoors freshness that eschewed the sense of entitlement of many attractive urban people her age.

"I wanted to come and see you just one last time." Jennifer saw the startled look in my eyes that her words provoked. "No, no, everything changed for the better. I wanted you to know . . . I mean, as you know, I worked at the hospice for a few months."

She took a deep breath, now recalling more fully that time one year ago. She folded her hands together on her lap, interlacing her long graceful fingers, and calmly said, "One of the men there—at the hospice—told me of his best friend who was also ill but was staying with his parents. They were looking for someone to help out with him."

I listened intently as she spoke. "So . . . he called his friend (since I told him I was interested in the job). He told Robert about me and even put me on the phone to talk to him.

"Anyway, Robert asked me to come over and I did. I talked with him for a couple of hours, then with his parents."

"John—that's Robert's father—" said Jennifer, "is a doctor so, at first . . . his father wasn't for it . . . because I didn't have a license or any technical training. But then, Robert told him about me caring for my mother at home with cancer and me being pre-med at college—up to my senior year, when I had to drop out because of personal problems."

"Pre-med?" I said, obviously surprised by the revelation.

Jennifer picked up on my reaction and spoke directly. "Well, at first it didn't seem important, given everything that was happening to me. Later," she sighed, "well . . . I guess I was embarrassed about it—with you having your degree and all."

"It's O.K.," I said reassuringly. "There was a lot going on for you." I paused, then said, "To come back to the family . . . it sounds as if you were feeling unsure about what was going to happen at that point—with Robert's father."

"Uh-huh. I was until his mother, Marge, began to talk. She wanted to know which pre-med courses I had taken, but mostly she wanted to know what kinds of things I did for my mother when was she was sick, and what kinds of things I did just to keep the house running," Jennifer explained. "I told them about the hospice, what I was doing and why I stayed there—that it meant a lot to me to help the guys."

"So Robert's mother got involved in the conversation, too?" I said.

Jennifer initially hesitated, wondering whether my comment had been a statement of fact or a question, but then went on. "So Marge turned to John and said, 'Why don't you and I hear from Robert to see what he thinks?' That's when they asked me to leave them alone for a while to talk. When I came back into the room, it was Marge who started the conversation by saying they were all comfortable with me, and asked me if I felt comfortable with them."

"I guess I must have smiled, because they all smiled. I told them I'd really like to work for them, and that was that. I've been there ever since.

"I felt guilty when I told Bernard I was leaving—especially after all he'd done for me, but he told me he understood and it was the right thing to do. He said I'd still be doing the same thing, helping someone. He just asked me to stay on for the week and to let the guys know I was leaving," said Jennifer.

"That—" she looked down, "that was the hardest part—along with not saying goodbye to you. But I kinda hoped you'd understand." She looked at me hoping,

I suspected, for a positive response from me.

"I can see you didn't reach that decision lightly," I said. "You'd been saying a lot of goodbyes." I paused, nodding my head. "I was a little disappointed, but Bernard did tell me you were O.K. and not to worry, so I was relieved to hear that," I said, smiling.

"Seeing you today is really nice. Also, to know things are much more positive for you now, that's good. But still, caring for Robert is—"

"Robert," Jennifer politely interrupted, "Robert died. He died the day after Christmas." Jennifer's eyes filled with tears and the tears began to run down her cheeks. She didn't attempt to wipe them away. She was obviously waiting until the emotion began to subside.

She cleared her throat. "That was terrible. I think in some manner, it was more difficult than when Mother died. My dad didn't show any feelings, nothing. So we just went through the motions, hardly talking . . . even when we buried her. Just went back to work and pretended nothing ever happened."

"You're saying Robert's death was different—harder on you—in some ways?"

Jennifer held from speaking, waiting again for her emotions to calm and for some measure of self-control to return. "Yes. Every day at their house, someone was saying, 'I love you'—and they meant it, too! They even said it to me."

I saw her difficulty containing the grief while verbalizing what she wanted to say. Nodding my head slowly, I said, "I see—"

"And it was awkward at first, hearing it. But eventually, I started to say, 'I love you' back to them. It wasn't phony or anything. It was real. I really began to feel it!

"There was so much love in the house, even with all of the suffering near the end, and so—" she hesitated, "so when he died, no one was saying it. No one was saying, 'I love you'—for so long."

"Not hearing those words for a long while sounds very painful for you, and yet, you continued to stay with Robert's parents afterward?"

Swallowing hard, she waited. When no longer able to contain the upwelling of emotion, she cried, "They wanted me. They wanted me!" Jennifer began to cry and, now wiping away the tears, she whispered, "They *really* wanted me."

Looking at me, she wiped away her tears and said, "Robert and I ended up knowing everything about each other. We didn't hold back any secrets. I think eventually he must have told his parents more about me because they just seemed to treat me differently after a while. Not bad, just more caring. They never said anything directly, but they let me know how much I meant to Robert and it meant everything to them. They said there was nothing I could say to them that would make them love me less.

"They said—" Jennifer inhaled deeply and let her breath out slowly. She seemed to be wondering whether I would believe what she was about to say. "They said I was always the sister he wanted and that really pleased them, that I took care of him just like he was my little brother and . . . and that they loved me . . . like—" Jennifer's eyes filled with tears, "they loved me like a daughter."

Straightening up in her chair, she continued, her voice slowly becoming firmer, overflowing with warmth and remembrance. "Way before Robert died, all of us would sit in the evenings, looking at their picture albums, homemade movies and slides. All of the old stories about him and his experiences and their experiences together, were shared and laughed about. Sometimes his dad would pretend to be angry and wag his finger at Robert, saying, 'I remember, young man, that one trip—I'm still angry at you for losing my fishing pole, letting it drift off, while you went after butterflies, Robert.'

"Robert would always say, 'Aww Dad, what'd ya expect? I liked pretty things. I still do.' And we'd all laugh."

"They even started making another album with pictures of all of us. When Robert was walking and still had the energy, we'd go out together—mostly with Marge. Oh," Jennifer added quickly, "with John, too, when he wasn't working. When Robert wasn't so sick, we'd make movies of all kinds of things, even silly things of us horsin' around."

"You all became close, very close," I said, "like a family."

"No one wanted to let go of him. It seemed if we just held on tight enough, it would last. Until . . . near the end. Then Robert let go. There was just no more fight left in him. We all stayed with him to the end. Then . . . it was over.

"Marge and I started crying, but John left the room. We got up and heard him in the bedroom. He was crying so hard. Finally, we went in and sat by his side. He reached out and pulled both of us to him and just held onto us so hard, like his heart was really breaking, and . , . we cried together."

I could see Jennifer choking back the tears. "We just all cried together for a long time."

I felt my own eyes begin to fill with tears. I was trying to find the words, struggling to express how deeply I was touched, when Jennifer went on.

"By the next day, there just didn't seem to be anything left in us. But things had to be done. His dad called to have Robert taken away. That was really hard. Then Marge and John had lots of other things to do. I took care of the house, answering the phone and preparing the meals, though nobody seemed to want to eat.

"Finally," she sighed deeply, "there was the memorial service with all of Robert's friends. Robert had a lot of friends. There were no other family members, except for an out-of-state cousin who came. Oh, one relative sent a card."

Jennifer paused. "Some people are . . . cruel. Others . . . others are thoughtless. In a way," she shrugged, "it's all the same. It's painful."

We both sat there silently.

Jennifer looked down at her hands on her lap, while I gazed to the side. I thought about her observation: the indifference of thoughtlessness and the cruelty of malice, each bringing pain in their wake. As I raised my eyes, Jennifer began to speak.

"I think that was really hard on Marge and John—the relatives. And some of their own friends, not wanting to come to the memorial service. I didn't say anything about that, but I understood. I mean, I know those kinda people. It didn't surprise me. But I really felt badly for Marge and John. They're really good people."

Jennifer began to fidget. I asked her if she'd like to stand up for a moment and stretch, knowing she tended to be a bit restless by nature. I knew she'd been used to being active and busy, and she probably reached a point where it seemed natural to do something. I also saw her look at the door, which let me know the session was coming to an end.

Jennifer stood up, clenched her hands and lifted her shoulders, stretching her athletic frame for a moment until she sat down again. "Anyway, I stayed on for the next couple of months.

"One evening, Marge and John asked me to sit down. They had something they wanted to say to me. They told me how much they appreciated everything I had done for Robert—and for them—that I had been so strong and had helped them through everything.

"I thought they were getting ready to let me go, but they told me I had become part of their family. They didn't want me to leave. They knew my life was more complicated than we had talked about, but none of that mattered to them. They told me again, they thought of me as their daughter and as Robert's sister.

"They wanted me to stay with them— to go back to school if I wanted to. They even told me if I was still interested in medicine, they would send me to either nursing or medical school. It's hard to believe, isn't it? But it's true!"

"No, Jennifer, it's not hard to believe. It sounds to me as if they really love and trust you," I said.

"Yes, they do. And I . . . I love them." Jennifer paused and sighed softly.

"I wanted to tell you my dad died in November. He left the ranch and everything to my husband and the kids. Todd started the divorce late last spring. He's got a girlfriend, Mary, an old friend of mine. She was never like the other people back there. She never cut me off. She told me Todd is coming around; he's not angry, just hurt and the kids really miss me. He lets me talk to them on the phone. It's real emotional, but he doesn't interfere with us talking.

"He's a good man. He was my first man—the only one. That's the way I got pregnant. We got married 'cause it was the right thing to do, but I never felt anything romantic for him. After a while, I just figured that's the way it is, the rest is all movies—not real life.

"So anyway, maybe after the divorce in June, Mary will bring the kids out for a visit. She's real warm-hearted. She keeps telling me not to worry, it'll all work out.

"I think one of the hardest parts," Jennifer said, nodding her head slowly, "was giving him custody of the kids, but I've got visitation rights, so we'll see. I felt it was best for the boys, not just because of my life out here, but because I want them raised on the ranch, and I know they've got a good home. I'll still get to see them."

"I'm sure that wasn't an easy decision for you, Jennifer. As someone special to me said about her family, *they're your blood,*" I said, thinking about Ruth and that evening together, gazing out over the forest.

"Yes, they are, for a fact! They are my blood."

I thought, *those words, 'they are, for a fact' are the same words Ruth would use at times.* Hearing the words, I felt them resonate deeply within myself and understood in that moment something basic about these two women and their relationship to the land and to their *blood*— their people.

"Yes," Jennifer said, "I think that I understand how strongly and deeply you feel about that."

"Well, I told John and Marge about everything. They said the kids are welcome—not to worry. It'll work out. They even joked they would now have grandchildren, which they never expected. You know," Jennifer looked at me and said earnestly, "They'll make great, really good grandparents for the boys.

"By the way, there's another reason I wanted to see you," Jennifer looked at me and I saw the genuine warmth and sincerity in her eyes. "I wanted to say how much I appreciate all you did for me. You saved my life."

She sensed I was a little uncomfortable with the praise and said quickly, "You know, it was while I was at the hospice that I saw those guys really wanted to live, but they had no choice. They were going to die. I realized I did have a choice. I could live or die, and it seemed so selfish of me to kill myself—no matter what the reason.

"Oh, yes," Jennifer paused, then said very seriously, "Joan killed herself, the woman I lived with in California."

I was surprised and found myself shaking my head in disbelief, "Joan killed herself? When?"

"Last September," she said.

"I saw her a couple weeks before that— by accident—at a store downtown. She came over to talk to me. I was feeling nervous, but I didn't want her to know it. So I tried just to stay normal.

"Joan wanted to know what I was doing. I told her I was living with a really great family, helping out and I was fine. It's strange," Jennifer seemed to be thinking aloud, dropping her eyes to her hands on her lap. "Joan had a smile on her face but," Jennifer looked up at me, "have you ever seen someone say nice things and at the same time when you look at their face it's all wrong? The face is just scrunched up, the eyes and the smile just look mean and angry, but she's still trying to put a smile on her face?

"Well," Jennifer seemed to shudder, "it's kinda spooky. Anyway, I saw a few weeks later in the newspaper where a doll maker died and was found in her house. I read that it was Joan, but no cause of death was listed. No family. No service.

"It sounds as if you felt a real shock about the news." I said.

"I did! I was shocked at first. It was hard to believe. Then, I don't know, I started wondering about it. I kinda had a strange feeling—I can't really describe it, but I needed to go over to her place. Well, I went over to the house and happened to see a neighbor I had been friendly with, and he told me the story.

"Joan left a note on the door, but no one came to the door and opened it, since Joan wasn't friendly with anyone in the neighborhood. It was the smell, I guess. She had been there for a while. This neighbor's dog kept going over to the door and whining. He went over and noticed the smell, too. He read the note, saying she was killing herself. He called the landlord, who went in and found her. There were a couple of bottles of sleeping pills next to her. That's what he said.

"A few days later," Jennifer continued, "I went out to the cemetery with some flowers. She told me where Janice and Rebecca were buried, that she had two more spaces next to them. She said one was for herself, but she didn't say who the other one was for."

Jennifer shook like she was trying to shake an insect off herself. "It was creepy. They were all there. I put the flowers on her grave and left. I thought about how that could've been me."

"What a very strange occurrence, Jennifer." I was thinking about the unusual turn of events, and all that Jennifer had seen and experienced the past year.

Perplexed, I said, "I'm not sure what it is, but something else is different about you. You . . . actually sound different somehow. It's hard for me to put my finger on it," I said, mystified.

"Oh, that! Remember, I told you about Joan criticizing the way I spoke, my accent and country speech? Well, I hated it when she did that. But when I came to Robert's and listened to the way they all spoke and how nice they sounded—even though they never made fun of me—well, I decided I wanted to speak like them. That's all.

"Don't ya worry, if I'm talkin' on the phone t' ma kids—dang!—it comes right on out. I palaver jus' like the best of 'em back there," she said, smiling.

"I see a lot has changed for you," I offered. "I am glad to hear that you're doing well, but am sorry to hear about Joan. I guess she was a very troubled person—not very stable or happy. John and Marge, they are really special, and you've got some good goals set for yourself, too."

That seemed to be the cue, both summarizing and ending our session. Jennifer stood up and shook my hand.

"Thanks again for everything. I'll stop by the desk and drop off a donation."

"Oh, by the way," Jennifer said, smiling and waving on the way out, "I'll be starting summer school in June." She hesitated for a moment, in the doorway and with her voice dropping softly, and said, "Thank you," and turned to walk out of the office.

Therapist Notes: Dr. Rauchenberg offered a theoretical interpretation: Joan's own suicidal ideation was masked and hidden from herself by denial and then projected by her onto Jennifer. Homicidal impulses and rage resulting from a history of loss, sexual abuse, betrayal, and an irrational belief that her lover was emotionally unavailable and un-supportive, fueled the unconscious desire to destroy her lover. Joan's coping skills failed her when she discovered Jennifer had not acted out the suicidal fantasy. As a result, Joan was left to act upon the suicidal impulse within herself, taking a lethal dose of barbiturates. It was, Rauchenberg maintained, rather like a boomerang flung outward and then returned to its owner.

AUTHOR'S NOTES

I had a general idea of what I wanted as a cover for *Homeless: The Dollmaker's Web*. Since the story was already written, it seemed like a relatively easy task of having an appropriate cover made by the designer. However, like so many creative projects, where you start and where you finish can have many permutations. This project was no different from front to end.

I brought my ideas and primitive sketches forward. There was a lot of back-and-forth between the two of us. Unbeknownst to me, the designer, after having read the novella, brought forward his own idea literally: he purchased a doll's head and photographed it, then provided background illustration. The cover was done. I had my cover.

Over a cup of tea, I was unexpectedly presented with the doll's head which, upon further examination, revealed the Star of David on the back of its head. According to the artist of that first portrayal of the doll's head, he had no idea the symbol was there when he purchased the doll. I had no intention at that time of discussing the matter of the symbol until a few years later when, after discussion with a Jewish friend, I felt readers would find it most interesting. Not only was the original manufacturer of the doll's head German, but the company that bought it as an attachment for the rest of the doll.

What struck me then and now were the improbabilities—the coincidence, if you will—that this particular doll's head with the Star of David would find its way to me.